I0587375

An EARL Like You

ANNA BRADLEY

OLIVERHEBERBOOKS

An Earl Like You Copyright 2025 © Anna Bradley

Cover art by Dar Albert at Wicked Smart Designs

Published by Oliver-Heber Books

0 9 8 7 6 5 4 3 2 1

PROLOGUE

The girls were singing again.

Singing. There was nothing to see for miles except for boring trees and boring meadows, and the scorching sun was burning an angry red patch into the back of his neck.

What was there to sing about? Not a thing that Cass could see, but those blasted girls had been out here every morning since he'd come to Kent, their high voices echoing in the still air.

It was aggravating, was what it was.

He hated it here. Kent was dull and ugly, and it was too bloody hot.

It was too hot to move. Too hot to breathe. It was so hot, even the dragonflies had given up their acrobatics and were turning in languid circles over the pond.

He kicked at the dried clump of grass with the heel of his boot.

What use was a hiding spot if those silly girls kept

pestering him with their stupid songs? He wanted to be alone. Was that asking too much? No one was ever pleased to see him, so he'd found a place where he could disappear, but even when he was invisible, he couldn't get any peace.

He kicked at the clump of grass again and a shower of dirt and pebbles flew off his heel, covering him with a dusty cloud of grime. Good. Hopefully his clothes were ruined. Mrs. Byrne, Lord Balfour's sour-faced housekeeper would scold, but she could nag until her face turned blue, and he wouldn't care. Why should he? She'd despised him from the moment his father's servant had left him on the doorstep. She'd hardly spared him a glance before her lips went so tight they turned white at the corners.

That was four days ago. Since then, no one had spoken a single word to him.

Not Lord Balfour, who was too preoccupied with his own concerns to spare a thought for the boy who'd been thrust upon him, and not Mrs. Byrne, who'd told the housemaids he was a sullen, scowling little hellion, and warned them to keep away from him.

He may as well have been a rabid dog, for all the welcome he'd gotten.

They didn't want him any more than his own father did.

Well, that was *fine* with him. He didn't give a toss about the opinions of some crusty old lord, especially not one who was friends with his father, who was a crusty old lord himself, and wicked, besides.

He didn't need his father, and he didn't need Lord Balfour, and he didn't need Mrs. Byrne, with her grim gray gowns and pinched lips.

He didn't need anybody.

All he needed was this tree. It was a good tree, with thick, low-lying branches that blocked the scorching sun and hid him from any curious eyes that happened to look in this direction.

It wasn't his tree, of course. It wasn't his pond, his shade or his dragonflies, any more than the great stone house on the top of the hill was his, or the formal gardens with the bright roses, their heavy heads nodding sleepily in the sun.

Nothing here was his.

Everything, from the bed he slept in at night to the pillow under his cheek belonged to Lord Balfour.

But not this tree. That was why he'd chosen it as his special hiding place.

The tree belonged to the gentleman whose estate bordered Lord Balfour's. He was a lord, too. There were lords everywhere out here in the country, by the looks of it. You couldn't toss a pebble without hitting some bloody useless viscount or earl.

The neighboring lord was called Lord Melton, or Lord Melrose, or something like that. It didn't matter what his name was. What mattered was Cass didn't owe Lord Balfour a single word of thanks for the branches above him or the turf underneath him.

It wasn't much, but it would have to do until his father decided what to do with him, and who knew how long that would take? A few weeks, maybe. Or maybe a few years.

Until then, there was nothing he could do to fill the long, tedious summer afternoons but swim in the pond, and hide in the shade of the tree.

Alone. He was always alone now, aside from the girls that came down to the pond every morning, but they didn't count, because they didn't know he was there, and even if they had, they wouldn't want to play with him.

No one here did.

Which was *fine* with him. Better than fine, because everyone knew girls' games were boring and stupid. He didn't want to play with them either, and if there'd been anyone around who dared to suggest otherwise, he'd have bloodied their noses for them, and blacked their eyes, too.

He knew how to fight. Every boy who'd come up in St. Giles could fight, and better than any prissy country boy, too. He was the best fighter in his mob, better even than some of the older—

"There are no more bluebells." The voice was no louder than a murmur, but it hung in the thick summer air. "Where have all the bluebells gone?"

Cass rolled onto his stomach and peeked through the tree branches. It was an excellent spying tree, with thick clusters of leaves and branches lying close to the ground. It was lowering, having to settle for spying on girls, but it wasn't as if he had anything better to do and, as Mrs. Byrne liked to say whenever he was in earshot, beggars shouldn't be choosy.

The girls were close, not more than five or six feet away. He could hear every word they said from his hiding place, which meant they could also hear him, so he mustn't give himself away with so much as a twitch or a deep breath.

There were three of them. One tall one, one medium one, and a small one who was always trailing behind the other two. He'd overheard one of the housemaids say they were Lord Melton's—or Lord Melrose's, or Lord Whoever-The-Devil-He-Was's—younger sisters.

The eldest one was Margaret, then there was Harriet, who was called Hattie, and then Sarah, who was a pale, sickly-looking thing, and not of much interest except that she was the proprietress of the picnic basket they brought with them, and there were nice-looking iced cakes in that basket that made his mouth water.

Aside from those cakes, the sisters were dull enough. They didn't do much aside from lie about chattering with each other. Sometimes Margaret and Hattie dipped their feet in the pond, but mostly they wandered around the meadow just beyond the spreading branches of his tree and picked flowers.

Flowers, of all stupid things. Who cared about flowers?

"It's sad when the bluebells are gone, isn't it?" The youngest one dropped down on the blanket her sisters had spread over the ground. She plucked a blade of grass from the parched patch of earth and began shredding it, the corners of her lips turned down. "I love the bluebells."

Margaret dropped down on the blanket beside her. "It's been ages since there were any bluebells, Sarah. It's too late in the year for them. But just look at all the daisies! Can't you content yourself with daisies?"

Sarah plucked up another blade of grass. "Daisies aren't *blue*."

"No, but cornflowers are." Hattie had thrown herself down on the blanket next to her sisters, but she leapt up again and brushed the grass from her skirts. "Bellflowers, too. Shall I go and find some for you?"

"Bluebells are ever so much prettier than cornflowers." Sarah's lower lip poked out. "Cornflowers are weeds."

"So are bluebells, and daisies too." Margeret stretched out on her back and threw an arm over her eyes. "Goodness, it's hot. Shall we swim, Hattie?"

"Later, perhaps. I'm going to pick some cornflowers for Sarah first."

"Don't bother. Why would I want a handful of weeds?"

Sarah's tone was so disagreeable, Cass clambered onto his knees so he could get a better look through the branches. Perhaps there'd be a brawl now. That would be something, wouldn't it?

But Hattie ignored her sister's fretfulness, saying only, "Because they're pretty."

Damn it. No brawl, then. He lay down again, his shirt sticking to his back and his scalp prickling with perspiration. Was it possible to die of boredom?

Margaret let out a yawn. "Go on, then. We'll swim when you get back."

Hattie wandered off, leaving her sisters to amuse themselves, and soon enough the monotonous buzz of the insects circling the pond lulled him into a doze.

He woke sometime later, his eyelids still heavy and so groggy it was as if his head had been stuffed with cotton wool.

Something had awoken him. A noise, high-pitched and joyful, like...

Laughter.

The girls were laughing, and all at once, he was irrationally, inexplicably angry, his blood boiling with fury. What did they have to laugh about? They were stuck here in the country without any friends and not a breath of cool air, and there wasn't anything they could do about it but lie here and stew in their own sweat.

What was so bloody amusing about that?

He struggled upright and peered through the space between the branches, all without making a sound. He was stealthy like that. He'd been chased enough times he knew how to keep still, to disappear while in plain sight.

If he didn't wish to be seen, he could remain invisible. No one had ever caught him out at it before.

Until now.

Because there, right on the other side of the branches, close enough he might have reached out and touched her was Hattie, the middle sister.

And she was looking right at him.

Her eyes were blue. A darker blue than the small bouquet of cornflowers she'd picked. The little clutch of them had been laid to one side of the picnic blanket in favor of dozens of daisies, their glowing yellow centers like tiny suns amidst the frothy white petals.

While he'd been napping, the girls had been making daisy chains. Their laps were overflowing with flowers, and each of them wore a cheerful crown of daisies woven amongst the bright golden locks of their hair. They were chattering and laughing, their voices floating high above the trees and brushing the edges of the wispy clouds in the sky until they became a part of the air itself.

He and Hattie stared at each other, his heart beating a wild tattoo in his chest, but she didn't speak to him, and after a moment he ducked back behind the branches and flopped onto his back with a thud.

Daisy crowns, of all stupid things. What use was a daisy crown? Even if he could have had one of his own, he wouldn't want it. He'd never liked daisies, anyway. He despised them, and he despised Kent, and he despised Lord Balfour and Mrs. Byrne, and he despised Lord Melrose's stupid sisters, too.

He despised this tree, and he was never going to come here again.

But most of all, he despised his father, because no matter how strong he was, or how clever he became, or how tall he grew, he wasn't ever going to be good enough for the Earl of Windham.

His mother was gone. She'd died several months ago, and he didn't have sisters or brothers. As for his father, he might as well not have had one at all, for all the attention the earl paid him.

He didn't have anyone.

The sisters packed up their basket and disappeared not long after that, back to their happy home where they probably did nothing but eat cakes and laugh together all day. It seemed much quieter after they'd gone. So quiet, his ears rang with silence, and his chest heaved with it.

When his eyes began to sting, he stumbled to his feet and dragged his arm across his damp cheeks before emerging from the shelter of the tree.

That was when he found it.

Just on the other side of the curtain of branches, so close he nearly stepped on it was a daisy crown, and beside it, wrapped in a cloth napkin was one of the cakes from the picnic basket, the white icing melting in the sun.

That was how it began, in the summer of eighteen-hundred and seven, the summer Cassian Fitzgerald turned eleven years old.

That was the summer he first laid eyes on Hattie Parrish. A summer of heat and dragonflies and the marshy scent of the pond, her shoulder touching his as they lay on their backs under Lord Melrose's ancient beech tree, the spreading branches swaying over their heads.

It was the best summer of his life, but he didn't know it, then.

He only realized it months later, after his father's servant came back for him, and he left Kent and Hattie Parrish behind.

But by then, it was too late.

By then, she was already a part of him.

ONE

COVENT GARDEN, LONDON, MARCH 1819

"I don't know how you do it, Windham. There isn't a gentleman in London who wins at the gaming tables as often as you do."

Cass let the door of The Deuce slam shut behind him. The heavy thud of the wood hitting the door frame echoed in the darkness around them, announcing their presence as surely as a pistol shot to any scoundrel who happened to be lurking in the shadows. That there was some version of scoundrel lurking nearby went without saying.

This was London, after all, but tempting fate had become one of his favorite pastimes.

"You've got the devil's own luck at Hazard." Hayward shoved his hands into his pockets and began to make his way down Maiden Lane as if he were taking a stroll down Rotten Row during the fashionable hour instead of skulking about the darkened streets of Covent Garden. "I've never seen anything like it."

"How dare you, Hayward? It's skill, not luck."

"Skill, at Hazard?" Hayward snorted. "I think not, my friend. But you don't look pleased, Windham. Indeed, for a man who just left a gaming hell several hundred pounds richer than when he entered it, you look downright grim."

"I don't care about the money." Cass fingered the stack of notes he'd tucked into his coat pocket. "Only a fool frequents the gaming hells expecting to get rich."

"Only a fool frequents gaming hells at all, but you're hardly a stranger at The Deuce. Everyone from the banker to the lowliest clerk greets you by name."

"One might say the same of you, Hayward."

"Yes, well someone has to keep an eye on you, don't they?"

Alas, there was no disputing that, as much as he would have liked to, but the truth was Hayward had been pulling him out of one scrape after the next since their Eton days, much as a more responsible elder brother might have done, even after Cass's harmless boyish pranks had given way to a grown man's far more worrying vices.

It was a mystery why Hayward bothered with him at all anymore.

"I go to pass the time." Although there always seemed to be more of it, no matter how much of it he wasted. "What do you suppose has become of the carriage?"

He'd left it...somewhere.

Bedford Street, maybe. Or had it been St. Martin's Lane?

Damned if he could remember, but no matter. Massey would find them. He always did. The man was a magician when it came to locating lost earls, but then this wasn't

Cass's first jaunt through Covent Garden in the wee hours of the morning. Massey had had a good deal of practice.

Hayward let out a long-suffering sigh. "It's on Garrick Street. I swear, Windham, you'd lose your own head if it wasn't sitting on your—"

"Shhh, Hayward." Cass paused in the middle of the street, the hair on his neck prickling. "Did you hear something?"

"No." Hayward paused, glancing around them. "Like what?"

"It sounded like footsteps." He peered into the darkness. It was as thick as a blanket around them, only a few dim rays of moonlight peeking through the heavy layer of London haze, but every inch of his skin was thrumming, and his senses tingling with warning.

Someone was there in the darkness, waiting.

"I think someone followed us from The Deuce. Quickly, Hayward."

"I don't hear any—" Hayward broke off with a grunt and dropped onto his knees on the cobbles. "What the devil!"

"Hayward! Are you—" That was as far as he got before a thick, muscular arm snaked around his throat, jerking him off his feet.

"Don't. Bloody. Move."

Cass shifted, his muscles flexing instinctively, but the arm around his neck tightened like a noose and the man wrenched him backwards with such brutal force if he hadn't had his walking stick he would have landed on his knees on the filthy cobbles beside Hayward, who was grappling with a shadowy figure roughly the size of a tree.

Cass kept his feet, but it did him no good. When he tried to throw the arm off it pressed against his windpipe, choking him.

"Are you deaf, my lord? I said don't move." A blade appeared in the man's hand, the dull gleam of it winking in the dim light, and an instant later warm blood trickled down his neck. "You don't follow orders very well, Lord Windham."

Lord Windham. The villain knew him. This wasn't a random robbery then, but a planned attack. It wasn't good news.

"Secure the other one."

Beside him there was a thud, followed by another grunt from Hayward, and a familiar, cold fury settled like a ball of ice in his chest. By the sounds of it, the blackguard had just planted a fist in his friend's stomach.

"Now, there's no need to be ungentlemanly about this, eh, Windham?" The villain who had him by the neck cackled, and a puff of his fetid breath wafted into Cass's face, making him gag.

"Just give me the money like a good lord, and we'll take our leave."

That voice. There was something familiar about it...

"Don't be a fool, my lord. Reach into your pocket, easy like, and hand over those bank notes before your friend here gets hurt."

The voice...yes, he had it now. It was the man who'd been seated beside him at the Hazard table earlier. He was a big, brutish sort of fellow, and he hadn't been pleased to see his money disappearing into Cass's hands.

"And we'll have those dice too while you're at it, your lordship."

Dice? What did he...oh. The man was accusing him of cheating with false dice. "I don't have any bloody—"

"'Course you do, my lord. Do you take me for a fool?" A rough hand was shoving at him, tearing at his clothing and pushing into his pockets. "No one wins like that without cheating."

Beside him, Hayward let out another gasp and toppled forward, his forehead striking the cobbles with a sickening thud, and another surge of rage gripped Cass, twisting his stomach.

No. This wasn't going to happen. Not without a fight.

A second passed, then another. The man on top of him tensed, sensing an oncoming attack, but he was a second too late. Cass jerked his head forward then slammed it back, smashing the back of his skull into the man's nose. The blade skimmed his throat, but he'd thrown his attacker off balance, and it left only a shallow cut.

He didn't feel it. Not the pain, and not the blood, though it was more than a trickle now, the thick heat of it pooling in the hollow of his throat. He didn't hesitate, but slammed his head back a second time, aiming for the man's nose.

He hit his mark. The man was too skilled a fighter to be surprised into releasing the stranglehold he had on Cass's neck, but not so skilled it didn't slacken, the muscles in his forearm loosening just enough for Cass to wrench free of his hold.

He whirled around and pulled his arm back, ready to land a fist in his attacker's jaw, but before he could swing, the man lunged. His knife arced through the air and found its mark on Cass's arm. Fortunately, his coat caught the brunt of it, otherwise the knife would have slashed him to the bone.

The man was quick, and struck again at once, but this wasn't Cass's first brawl, and he was ready for him. He blocked the blow with his walking stick, then swung for the man's head, but his attacker leapt backward in time to avoid a strike to the temple that would have knocked him senseless.

Instead, the stick caught him in the chest in a blow that should have sent him crumpling to the ground, but he was a big, strapping fellow, and he only staggered backwards, a whoosh of air bursting from his lungs. He kept his feet, a bloodthirsty snarl on his lips and swung, and his meaty paw connected with Cass's cheek.

His head jerked sideways, the entire side of his face exploding in pain, but by some miracle he managed to stay upright. He circled the man, waiting for his chance, and when he saw an opportunity to strike, he lunged, throwing every bit of strength he had left in his body into the blow.

The man leapt to block him, but he was expecting Cass to aim for his head or chest again. Instead, Cass aimed for the vulnerable space behind the man's knees.

The blow was swift and brutal. The man's legs collapsed underneath him, and he went down like a horse, his body weight sending him slamming into the cobbles. He kept hold of his knife, but before he could move Cass was straddling him, his knees digging hard enough into the man's sides to make him gasp.

Cass tossed his walking stick aside and seized the man's

wrist. He slammed it as hard as he could against the cobbles beneath them, but the man didn't drop his weapon. So, Cass did it again, then again, until his attacker's fingers went slack around the knife's hilt.

He seized the knife, and God only knows what he might have done with it, how far he might have taken it, but before he could move, something slammed into the side of his head.

Pain burst inside his skull—splitting, searing pain—and stars burst behind his eyelids.

Then he was falling, his vision tunneling as he plummeted into darkness.

"If you insist upon winning exorbitant amounts of money at the Covent Garden gaming hells, Windham, then you'd do well to remember where you left your carriage."

Something was moving in front of Cass's face, but black was crowding at the edges of his vision, and he couldn't make out what it was. "Is that you, Hayward?"

"Yes. Who else would it be? Take my hand."

Hand? What...oh. That's what that blurry thing in front of him was. Cass grasped the hand Hayward offered and stumbled to his feet, gritting his teeth against the throbbing pain in his temple.

"Do you know what happens when you *don't* recall where you left your carriage, Windham?"

Cass glanced around, but the men who had attacked them were long gone, and with them the three hundred pounds that had been in his pocket. "No, but I have a feeling you're going to tell me."

"You get set upon by blackguards, that's what. We're damn lucky we didn't get our throats slit." Hayward drew his fingers across his neck with a dramatic flourish.

Cass rolled his eyes. Hayward had a lecture for every occasion, each one of them as helpful as the next. Which was to say, not helpful at all.

"What an invaluable lesson, Hayward, if a bit after the fact." Cass fumbled in his coat pocket for his handkerchief and handed it to his friend. "Here. Your nose is bleeding."

"You made quick work of that one villain." Hayward pressed the handkerchief to his nose, chortling with obvious relish. "I daresay he wasn't expecting such a dirty fight from a proper earl like yourself."

An earl, yes. Proper? Hardly.

"If you recall, Hayward, I spent a good part of my child-hood in St. Giles. This wasn't my first street brawl." The *ton* might snicker about his low birth, but a childhood spent scrapping with ruffians did come in handy now and again.

"A good thing, too, or else those two would have carved us up like a pair of Christmas geese. Have you ever consid-ered going into prizefighting, Windham? You could make money and scandalize the *ton* at the same time."

The side of Cass's face was on fire, his chest ached as if a horse had trod on it, and bits of his brain were likely oozing from his ear, but he couldn't stifle the hoarse laugh that broke from his lips. "The last I remember, I was about to introduce that blackguard to the business end of his blade, but something hit me."

"It was your walking stick." Hayward picked it up from where it lay on the cobbles. "If he hadn't gotten ahold of it, you would have bested him, but a wee tap to the skull, and you toppled over like a sack of potatoes. They had the money by then, and fled into the night like the scoundrels they are, and thank goodness they did, or else we—"

"Is this going to be a long lecture, Hayward? Because I'm rather busy, what with the bludgeoning and all. Shall we go and find Massey before another pair of scoundrels appears? I've had quite enough entertainment for one night."

"Are you sure you can manage it?" Hayward ran a doubtful glance over him. "You're a bit unsteady on your feet, and you look like you've been beaten with a stick."

"I *have* been beaten with a stick." Cass waved at the walking stick still clutched in Hayward's fist. "Remember?"

"So, you have. Very well, then." Hayward took his arm and led him toward Garrick Street, and there under the light of a gas lamp was his carriage, right where they'd left it, with Massey perched atop the box.

There wasn't another servant in London—or quite possibly in all of England—who was more impassive than Massey. The man had been a witness to enough scandals during his tenure with Cass's father that nothing shocked him anymore.

But even Massey raised an eyebrow when he got a look at Cass's rapidly swelling eye, and the blood trickling from Hayward's nose. "All right, my lords?"

"Never better, Massey." But Cass let out a groan as he stumbled up the steps and collapsed against the squabs.

What had that villain done to his ribs? His entire left side was throbbing as if it were on fire.

It was only a short distance from Covent Garden to his townhouse in Berkeley Square, but a lifetime seemed to pass as they made their way through the silent London streets. By the time they arrived his head was swimming again, and Hayward was obliged to help him alight from the carriage.

"Straighten my coat and tidy my hair, will you, Hayward?"

"Tidy your hair!" Hayward gaped at him as if he'd lost his wits. "Am I to be your lady's maid now, Windham?"

"Come, Hayward, help make me more presentable. I don't want to upset Mrs. Hughes." His housekeeper was a tender-hearted soul, and all the blood and bruising might send her into a fit of hysterics.

"Presentable? I think that's closing the barn door after the horse has fled, Windham." But then he noticed Cass was cradling his right hand against his chest, and he let out a heavy sigh. "Did you twist it?"

"Yes, when that blackguard tackled me, I put out my hand to stop my fall."

"Ah. Well, I suppose it could have been worse. That was a six-inch blade he had in his hand. We're fortunate your head is still attached to your neck."

Cass didn't feel particularly fortunate, but he said nothing as Hayward made a few adjustments to his person, grumbling the entire time. "All right then, there you are. Pretty as a sunrise."

Cass rolled his eyes as they trudged up the steps toward the front door, but it flew open before they could touch the knob, and there stood Mrs. Hughes. She'd clearly been awaiting their return, the dim light of the hallway sconces behind her lighting up her silver hair like a halo.

The light fell across Cass's face, and she lifted her hand to her mouth with a gasp. "Lord Windham! And Lord Hayward, my goodness! What's happened?"

"It's all right, Mrs. Hughes," Cass began, even as he knew his words would fall on deaf ears. As far as Mrs. Hughes was concerned, blood was never all right.

"Not to worry, Mrs. Hughes," Hayward added. "He'll be all right. Windham here has the hardest head of anyone I've ever encountered."

Mrs. Hughes drew herself up with terrifying dignity. "I beg your pardon, my lord, but Lord Windham is most certainly *not* all right. He looks as if he's been run down by a barouche!" She backed away from the door, waving them inside. "I'll send for Dr. Champion at once."

"No doctors, if you please, Mrs. Hughes." Cass limped through the door with Hayward on his heels, Mrs. Hughes clucking over them both like a hen over a pair of baby chicks. "A rest will set me right again."

Mrs. Hughes stared at him, aghast. "But you're *bleeding*, and your eye is turning black. You were gallivanting around Covent Garden again, weren't you? For pity's sake, will you never learn, my lord?"

If she'd been another one of his servants, he wouldn't have tolerated such insolence, but Mrs. Hughes had been his father's housekeeper as well. She'd known him since he was a boy of eleven years and had come to live with his father in this very townhouse, and she'd been kind to him, even when all the other servants were whispering behind his back.

She'd been kinder to him than his father ever had been. She was the closest thing he'd had to a mother since his own mother had died, and in his eyes, she could do no wrong.

He wasn't a good man. That much was plain. But he was loyal, and he never raised his voice to Mrs. Hughes, no matter how much she scolded.

"Finley, come here at once and see to his lordship." Mrs. Hughes beckoned to a footman waiting in the shadows. He was a big Irish lad who'd performed this service for Cass more than once before. "Help him up the stairs, Finley."

"Aye, Mrs. Hughes." Finley sprang forward. "All right there, my lord?"

"I daresay I'll survive, Finley." He'd had worse, but his head was throbbing, he could no longer see out of his injured eye, and he was struggling to keep his feet underneath him.

"Take him to his bedchamber, Finley. Now then, Lord Hayward..."

Cass made his way up the stairs, leaning heavily on Finley, chuckling as Mrs. Hughes cajoled, bullied and then ordered Hayward up to the blue bedroom in the guest wing. The Albany wasn't far, but Mrs. Hughes wouldn't hear of Hayward setting foot outside the door again that night.

But later, as he lay alone in his bed, his ribs aching and his eye swollen shut, the incident was a good deal less amusing.

He'd persuaded himself it would be different this time. He was the Earl of Windham now, and London aristocrats adored their earls, particularly the wealthy ones.

But this was no different than St. Giles had been, or Eton, or later, Oxford.

The *ton* tolerated him, but he'd never truly be one of them. He didn't fit here any better than he did anywhere else.

He'd only ever found his footing once. That had been more than a decade ago, and that time, that place, and that friend was lost to him now.

As lost as if they'd never existed.

TWO

MELROSE HOUSE, KENT, EARLY MAY

"Did you fetch my silk ribbons, Hattie?" Sarah mumbled around a mouthful of pins as Hattie entered the small parlor with her marketing basket over her arm.

"Silk ribbons? No." She stripped off her gloves and set them down on the table beside the door. "Was I meant to?"

"For pity's sake, Hattie! I asked you to—"

"Kindly remove those pins from your mouth before you speak, Sarah." Margaret glanced up from the book she'd been reading. "I don't wish to explain to Dr. Paulson how you managed to swallow half a dozen sewing pins. He already thinks we're mad as it is."

"Oh, hang Dr. Paulson! What do I care what he thinks?"

"I daresay you'll care when those pins are lodged in your throat," Margaret said mildly. "I can't think it would be at all pleasant. Rather like swallowing a cactus."

Sarah plucked the pins from between her lips, dropped them onto the table beside her chair and turned to glower at

Hattie. "I asked you to fetch four yards of violet silk ribbon from the mercantile to trim my new straw bonnet."

Dash it, she had, hadn't she? That is, Sarah had shouted *something* to her from the doorway as she'd made her way down the pathway that led to the tiny village of Chatham, and it was just as likely to have been about ribbons as anything else. "Oh, dear. I beg your pardon, Sarah. I forgot."

"Honestly, Hattie, you may as well let Molly do the marketing if you're going to be so forgetful." Sarah tossed the unfinished bonnet onto the table with a tragic sigh. "I was going to wear that bonnet when I called on Mrs. Lyons today, but I can't possibly wear it without the violet ribbon."

"I truly am sorry. Perhaps this will cheer you up." Hattie rummaged inside her basket and pulled out a letter. "Alice Weatherby has written to you from London."

"Another letter already?" Sarah held out her hands, brightening at once. "Look, it's a lovely long one. What a pity Alice is leaving London at the end of the week, just when the season is about to begin. There's sure to be one delicious scandal after another, and no one to report it."

"Dear me, whatever shall we do without an endless flow of gossip from London?" Margaret turned over a page of her book. "What will become of us?"

"I know. It's tragic, is it not?" Sarah huffed. "Alice has all the best gossip."

Hattie stifled her sigh as she dropped into her chair opposite the window. Alice had been as faithful a correspondent as she'd promised Sarah she would be.

Far more faithful than certain other people, despite the promises they'd made.

She'd had such high hopes when Mr. Briggs, the post-master had handed her the letter this morning, only to have them immediately dashed. Cass hadn't written to her since last October, and the eight months since she'd received his last letter felt like an endless, lonely walk through a barren desert.

Eight long months, and this despite the dozens of letters she'd sent him during that time. At first, she'd put his silence down to his father's illness, but the Sixth Earl of Windham had drawn his last breath nearly four months ago, and still she hadn't heard a word from Cass.

Perhaps he no longer had time for her. He was the earl now, after all, handsome, elegant, and wealthy, and she... well, she was who she'd always been. Harriet Parrish, the quietest of Lord Melrose's three reclusive sisters. No one special. A spinster in the making. Certainly not the sort of lady who could hold the attention of a fashionable earl like Lord Windham.

"Ooh, listen to this! Alice says Mr. Allan and Lord Fullerton were spotted stumbling about the streets outside of Brooks's Club in the wee hours of Monday morning!"

"There's nothing so scandalous in that, surely?" Margaret turned over another leaf of her book. "Don't all the most fashionable gentlemen frequent Brooks's Club?"

"They do, yes, but it seems Lord Fullerton had been dipping rather deep that evening, and..." Sarah let out a gasp. "My goodness! Alice says Mr. Allen accused Lord Fullerton of cheating at whist, and Lord Fullerton responded by issuing Mr. Allen a challenge to a duel! Dear me, London is terribly exciting, isn't it?"

"Exciting? No. Scandalous and disgraceful, yes." Margaret snapped her book closed and set it aside. "I do wish Alice weren't quite so fond of gossip."

"Indeed. I can't imagine it does you any good, reading about such nonsense, Sarah." Hattie rose, marched across the room and snatched her book of pressed flowers down from the bookcase. "For my own part, I don't care a fig for the scandals of London's fashionable aristocrats."

Sarah ignored this and continued reading, breathless with excitement. "Lord Henry and his brother, Viscount Golding, were seen entering Madame White's, a notorious brothel in the Strand in the wee hours of Sunday morning. They emerged some hours later in the company of a pair of birds of paradise, and—"

"For pity's sake!" Hattie slammed the heavy book onto the table, making Sarah and Margaret jump. "No brothels, and no birds of paradise, if you please, Sarah."

"You needn't make such a fuss, Hattie. I know all about birds of paradise." Sarah gave a nonchalant wave of her hand. "*Chère amies*, too. Alice says all the fashionable gentlemen have them."

"That's quite enough, Sarah."

Sarah glanced up from her letter at Margaret's stern tone, her cheeks coloring. "I beg your pardon. I'll just read to myself, shall I?"

"Yes, I think that would be best." Margaret opened her book again and a companionable quiet settled over the parlor.

It should have soothed Hattie's jangled nerves, but instead she found herself staring down at her book, the colorful page of pressed larkspurs swimming before her eyes.

Perhaps she'd been a fool to believe she and Cass would always be friends. She hadn't seen him since the summer he'd come to Kent. That had been twelve years ago, and with every subsequent year that passed it seemed less likely she'd ever lay eyes on him again.

But for him to just go silent as he'd done, with no warning or explanation felt like…her heart gave a sharp throb of pain in her chest, as if it had been speared with a dagger.

If felt like betrayal. Or worse, abandonment.

But then if the scandal sheets were to be believed, he spent his every waking hour engaged in one debauchery after another. Apparently, it was rather time-consuming, being a wicked, dissipated earl, and left him little leisure to write.

Not that it mattered much anymore. It was just as well he'd ended their correspondence, as it wasn't proper for a lady to write to a gentleman to whom she wasn't betrothed. Her brother would have worried if he'd known of it, and she didn't like to lie to Johnathan, or go behind his back.

Cass was doubtless taken up with his fashionable friends at Brooks's, and his *chère amie*, and…and…well, whatever it was young aristocratic gentlemen got up to in London.

Yes, it was much better this way. She'd forget all about him soon enough, and the good news was she'd have much more time to devote to her flowers now. Really, it was a tremendous relief to be free of such arduous correspondence.

A tremendous relief, indeed.

She turned to a blank page in her book and plucked up the white larkspur she'd picked several weeks ago. She'd dried it between two sheets of the special absorbent paper Johnathan had brought her from London, so the white petals wouldn't turn yellow after it was pressed.

It was ready now, and she had the perfect place for—

"Goodness, that's...oh, my."

Hattie turned to Sarah, her hand going still over the thick book spread out on the table in front of her, and her heart plummeted from her chest into her slippers at the stricken look on her sister's face. "What is it?"

Except she knew. Even before Sarah said a word, she knew.

"It seems, ah...well, it sounds as if Cassian has got himself into a bit of a scrape."

"What scrape?" Hattie's voice was much higher than it should have been, and her cheeks went hot as Sarah's and Margaret heads jerked toward her. "What's he done this time?"

"Perhaps it would be best if we—" Margaret began, but Hattie interrupted her.

"No. I want to hear it. Read it, Sarah."

Her sisters exchanged a glance, but then Sarah began reading in a halting voice. "Cassian Fitzgerald, the newly minted Earl of Windham was seen stumbling down Maiden Lane after a street brawl near The Deuce in Covent Garden."

"A brawl?" Margaret let out a breath. "What, another one?"

"It seems so, and this one must have been quite a melee. Listen to this. Lord Windham's friend Lord Hayward—"

"Lord Hayward!" Margaret exclaimed. "Stephen Beaumont, the Earl of Hayward?"

"Alice doesn't say, but I suppose there's only one Lord Hayward, isn't there?" Sarah resumed reading. "Lord Windham's friend Lord Hayward, who was bleeding profusely from his nose, was obliged to assist his unsteady companion from Maiden Lane to Garrick Street, where Lord Windham's carriage and driver were waiting. Lord Windham was staggering, either from an excess of drink or a nasty blow he sustained to his temple."

The stem of the larkspur she was holding snapped between Hattie's fingers.

Margaret let out a breath. "Dear God. What can Cass be thinking, brawling in public in such a disgraceful manner?"

Hattie stared down at the broken flower cradled in her palm until it blurred in front of her eyes. Silly of her, to get so upset over it. She could replace it easily enough. There were dozens of white larkspurs in the Melrose House gardens.

She could pick another one. One was as good as another—

"Lord Windham's left eye was swollen shut, and according to our witness he collapsed as soon as he gained his carriage."

She was going to be sick. She pressed a hand to her abdomen as if she could push back the nausea welling there.

"Sarah." Margaret glanced at Hattie. "Perhaps the less said about Cassian's antics, the better."

"Yes, of course. I beg your pardon." Sarah hastily folded the letter and stuffed it into the pocket of her dress. "I'm certain it's all lies in any case, or at the least a wild exaggeration. One can't trust what one reads in the scandal sheets."

It was no lie. They all knew it, but none of them had the heart to say it, and a heavy silence descended on the drawing room.

What was there to say? Not a word, and there was even less she could do about it. It wasn't as if she could rush off to London. She wasn't fond of society. She despised the dirt and noise of Town and avoided it like the plague. She hardly ever ventured outside of her quiet little corner of Kent.

"I believe I'll go for a walk." She jumped to her feet, tipping the table askew in her haste to get away. "It's a lovely day."

It wasn't. The sky was overcast, and a chilly wind had arisen in the last hour, rustling the treetops, but neither Sarah nor Margaret contradicted her. Margaret said only, "Wear your cloak, won't you, dear?"

"I will." Hattie dropped the broken larkspur into the pocket of her dress. "I'm just going to the east garden. I won't be long."

This reassurance did nothing to erase the anxious furrow from Margaret's brow. Hattie hated worrying her sisters, but all at once the walls of the drawing room were closing in on her, and she couldn't bear to sit still for another minute.

The fresh air would set her right again. Of course, it would. A few deep breaths would chase Cass's ghost out of her head.

But she hadn't taken more than a half dozen steps down the corridor before Margaret's low murmur made her pause. "Cassian's situation seems to grow worse with every day that passes. One can't pick up a scandal sheet without seeing his name on the front page."

Hattie eased closer to the drawing room door, pressing against the wall so she wouldn't be seen if Sarah or Margaret happened to glance toward the corridor.

She *wasn't* eavesdropping. No, nothing so low and tawdry as that. She was merely curious, that was all.

"Yes, I'm afraid that's so." Sarah let out a heavy sigh. "He's become the spitting image of his father, hasn't he? It's such a pity. It hardly seems possible such a lovely boy as Cass could have become such a disappointing man."

"On the contrary, it's entirely possible, especially with such a father as he had. Even before he inherited the title, Cass had too much money, too much freedom, and a father who set the worst possible example for him."

"Indeed. He really had no chance, did he?"

"No, and though I hate to be a harbinger of doom, with the way the aristocratic gentlemen carry on in London, I'm afraid it will only get worse."

Worse? Hattie hovered in the corridor, her heart crowding into her throat. How could it possibly get worse than gaming and bloody, drunken brawls? But then Margaret was right. London was full of temptations, especially for a gentleman who had a title and plenty of gold coins in his pockets.

At least, he did for now. The Windham coffers were deeper than most, but more than one young, reckless aristocrat had lost their fortune at London's gaming tables, and if the scandal sheets had the right of it, Cass spent an inordinate amount of time wagering.

How long? How long would it take before he was utterly ruined? How long before he wasn't Cass anymore? Not *her* Cass, the Cass she remembered, who'd once brought her handfuls of wildflowers and sat with her under the beech tree. The boy who'd spent hours stringing daisy chains with her, and who'd written her letters from Eton, and then later from Oxford.

How long would it take before there was nothing left of that sweet, sensitive boy? Had his father bled every ounce of tenderness and compassion from him?

She had no answers. Just the darkening sky above her, the patter of raindrops on her head, and the whispers of Cass's ghost in her ears.

The wind grew sharper, yet she wandered on until the hems of her skirts were soaked, and her slippers were ruined.

"Hattie? Hattie, wait!"

She turned to find Margaret hurrying toward her, holding her hat down with one hand, her skirts whipping in the wind. "My goodness, Hattie! Didn't you hear me? I've called your name a dozen times."

"Did you, indeed? I beg your pardon. I was distracted, I suppose." She mustered a smile for her sister, but it was a poor, thin thing, stiff and awkward on her lips.

"Why are you walking in the rain?" Margaret came to a breathless stop beside her. "You'll catch your death out here."

"Is it raining?" She glanced up into the gloomy sky. Fat raindrops fell from the clouds and spattered her cheeks. "I didn't notice."

"Come inside, Hattie. It's time for tea."

Teatime, already? It was much later than she'd thought. Despite her promise not to linger outdoors, she'd been wandering the gardens for hours.

"Hattie." Margaret took her hand and gave it a comforting squeeze. "Are you all right?"

Was she? She didn't know anymore.

Margaret peeked under the wide brim of Hattie's bonnet and her face fell. "Oh, my dear girl. Walk with me and tell me about it."

They turned down a path that led toward the house, and she opened her mouth to pour her heart out to the sister she loved and trusted more than anyone else in the world but then closed it again without a word passing her lips.

Her thoughts were all tangled in her head. How could she explain that even though so many years had elapsed since that magical summer she and Cass had spent underneath the low branches of the beech tree, he still haunted her thoughts?

It was absurd, ridiculous that so brief a friendship still had the power to overset her, and yet...

And yet, here they were.

How could she ever explain it to Margaret in a way that made sense? How could she speak of him when the mere thought of him made her chest tight and tears sting her eyes? If she ventured a single word about Cass right now, she'd burst into tears.

It wasn't that Margaret would laugh at her. Her sister would never do something so cruel, but her heart was tender today, bruised and battered, and she'd never felt more useless in her life.

ANNA BRADLEY

Cass seemed to be determined to ruin himself, and there wasn't anything she could do to stop it. If she could only talk to him, perhaps she could shake some sense into him, but he was in London, and she was stuck here in Kent.

Although was she truly stuck? She *could* go to London, but if she did, what would she say to him? How could she make Cass listen to her? He'd cared for her friendship once, yes. She had no doubt of that, but it had been years ago, and if she scandal sheets were to be believed, the man he'd become was nothing like the boy he'd once been.

But could she ever forgive herself if she didn't try?

"Hattie?" Margaret laid a hand on her sleeve, bringing them both to a halt on the pathway and gazed at her with anxious blue eyes. "Are you unwell? You look strange."

"I'm very well, I assure you. I was just wondering if..."

Did she dare? She wasn't brave, not like Sarah, but the thing was, even if Cass was no longer *her* friend, she was still *his*.

"Yes? Wondering what?"

She sucked in a deep breath and leapt over the precipice. "The Royal Horticultural Society is doing a series of lectures over the next few weeks. I thought...well, I thought perhaps I might attend."

Margaret blinked. "But the Royal Horticultural Society is in *London*."

"Yes, I'm aware of that." Despite her misery, a laugh fell from her lips. "That's why some people call it The Royal *London* Horticultural Society."

"No one calls it that. I believe you're thinking of the

London Royal Hospital. Or the London Royal Opera House. Or the London Royal Ballet, or—"

"Yes, never mind. Sir Joseph Banks is meant to deliver a lecture this year, and the man is eighty years old if he's a day. If we don't hear him this time, we may never have another chance."

Margaret frowned. "Since when are you so enamored of Sir Joseph Banks? This is terribly sudden, Hattie."

"It's not, really. I've been thinking of going for some time now." It was a bald-faced lie, and her cheeks heated with shame, but she managed to hold Margaret's gaze.

"Johnathan and Emmeline won't like it." Margaret hesitated, then added, "If they find out."

"They won't find out. We'll be there and then back again before they return from Oxfordshire." Johnathan and Emmeline had gone to Hawke's Run to spend time with Emmeline's sister Helena and Helena's husband Adrian until Helena was delivered of her second child.

"Let me make sure I understand you, Hattie. You're saying you want to go to London?"

Margaret's eyebrows had risen into her hairline, as well they might. Hattie had never shown the least inclination to venture into London before this. She'd always been happy to remain in Kent with her flowers and her sisters to keep her company.

But Kent would be here waiting for her when she returned.

"Yes. I want to go to London, but how is the thing to be managed?" They'd have to go without a chaperone, and they couldn't stay at the townhouse in Grosvenor Street without Johnathan finding out about it.

"A bit tricky, isn't it, especially this close to the start of the season." Margaret tapped her lip, thinking, then gave a decisive nod. "There's only one lady in England who can see it done properly."

"Who?"

Margaret's lips curved in a grin. "Lady Fosberry, of course."

THREE

BERKELEY SQUARE, LONDON, ONE WEEK
LATER

T he scent of pineapple ices was making him ill.

"What the devil is wrong with you, Windham?" Hayward turned away from the carriageful
of ladies they were waiting on and lowered his voice. "Good
Lord, man, but you're a bit green about the gills. I hope
you're not going to cast up your accounts in front of half the
ton. It's not at all the thing."

"I don't understand the appeal of pineapple ices." Cass
retrieved his wrinkled handkerchief from the breast pocket
of his coat and pressed it to his nose. "The smell is
nauseating."

"Smell? I don't smell anything. Perhaps a touch of elderflower sugar, but that's all."

"The elderflower is fine, but the pineapple smells sour,
like vinegar." Or was that his handkerchief? He raised the
limp linen to his nose again, took a cautious sniff, then
hastily stuffed it back in his coat pocket.

"Don't let Gunter hear you say so. Bad for business, you know."

"Gunter has nothing to worry about." Cass nodded at the phaetons, gigs and the occasional barouche crowding Berkeley Square, their fashionable passengers all chattering and laughing at once, colorful ices in elegant silver cups clutched in their hands.

The season was upon them, and there was no place in London where that was more evident than outside Gunter's Tea Shop in the afternoon. The *ton* loved nothing more than flaunting their finery on the promenade before flocking to Gunter's afterwards to indulge in ices and gossip.

"Perhaps it isn't the ices making you ill, Windham, but the quantity of brandy you drank at Lord Chapman's soiree last night."

"It's not the brandy."

That is, it *was* the brandy, but not *just* the brandy. It was the cheroots, too, and the hours spent wagering with Chapman, who'd taken no less than four hundred pounds off him. He hadn't returned to his townhouse until the wee hours of this morning, then he'd slept the entire day and been obliged to rush through his toilette to make it to Hyde Park in time to escort Lady Laetitia down the promenade during the fashionable hour.

Hence the disgraceful state of his linen.

But the pineapple ices didn't help matters. The bile was gurgling in the back of his throat, threatening at every moment to overflow his lips, and his hands weren't quite steady.

"The ladies must have their ices, Windham." Hayward

nodded at the carriage where Lady Laetitia, this season's undisputed belle, was whispering to her two companions. "No proper gentleman would dream of depriving the ladies of their little indulgences."

No one, neither gentleman nor lady would dream of depriving Lady Laetitia of a single thing she desired. Alas, what Lady Laetitia desired above all else was to be seen outside Gunter's Tea Shop, holding court over her friends while all the most elegant gentlemen danced in attendance upon her. It was the most fashionable place to be on a sunny afternoon in May, and God knew they all must be fashionable, or die.

When had this all become so tedious? He'd enjoyed it at first, hadn't he? The balls and routs and soirees, his box at the theater and lunches at White's followed by hours of clandestine wagering at the gaming hells—it had all been entertaining enough when he'd taken his place in society as the Seventh Earl of Windham, hadn't it?

But that was the trouble with shiny things. They paled quickly, and the blush had most certainly worn off the rose of the Windham peerage. No wonder his father had been such a delinquent. One had to do *something* to alleviate the boredom of being an earl.

A high-pitched giggle burst upon the air, and he and Hayward turned toward the carriage where Lady Laetitia was enthroned upon pale blue velvet squabs. If the gossips were to be believed, her father Lord Tremblay had chosen that specific shade of blue because it complemented his precious Laetitia's blue eyes.

Those blue eyes were currently the toast of London, and

they were pretty enough, despite being the wrong shade of blue. They were forget-me-not-blue, instead of bluebell blue—

"All right there, ladies?" Hayward gave the smiling trio a courtly bow, eliciting another shrill giggle from the young ladies that pierced Cass's feeble defenses, lancing through his eyeballs directly into his skull.

Good Lord, but his head was pounding. This was all Chapman's fault. A curse upon the man and his free-flowing brandy.

"Come now, Windham." Hayward nudged him. "You look as grim as an undertaker, and on such a lovely day, and with such a vision of beauty before us, too. The ladies look particularly picturesque in the sunlight, do they not?"

"They're well enough, I suppose." But not nearly as picturesque as his darkened bedchamber would have been.

Hayward raised a brow. "Damned with faint praise, indeed. You'll have to do better than that if you want to secure Lady Laetitia, Windham."

That was the trouble. He didn't care one whit whether he secured Lady Laetitia or not, but he fixed a dutiful smile over his clenched teeth, nonetheless. It wouldn't do to spend all afternoon scowling at the lady he was meant to be courting.

The match with Lady Laetitia had been his father's idea. In fact, he'd insisted on it, but of course his father was in no position to demand anything now, being dead and comfortably ensconced inside a thick marble slab in the family tomb.

But if Cass must marry—and he must, as he was the Earl of Windham now—then what difference did it make which lady he made his countess? Lady Laetitia would do as well as any of the others.

Better than any of them, if one took her fortune into consideration, which his father certainly had. The Windham earldom was a wealthy one, but no amount of money had ever been enough for his father, and Lord Tremblay's land bordered the Windham country property in Oxfordshire.

Joining the Windham and the Tremblay names would mark the beginning of the empire his father had always dreamed about. There was a great deal of money to be made if he and Lady Laetitia wed—enough money that a match between them was as good as decided, despite his indifference toward her.

The *ton* expected it, and they must appease the *ton*, or die.

"Lord Windham? Yoo-hoo, Lord Windham?" Lady Laetitia beckoned to him with an imperious wave of her hand. "A word, if you'd be so kind?"

"Go on, Windham." Hayward gave him a none-too-gentle push toward the carriage. "And attempt a smile, would you? It won't do to look as if you're approaching the gibbet when you speak to your future bride."

"At least a man can have some peace after a visit to the gibbet." But he did as he was told and straightened from the railing, pasting a smile on his face as he walked toward the carriage. "Lady Laetitia. Have I told you how lovely you look this afternoon?"

"No, you have not, my lord. Why, you've hardly spoken a dozen words to me since we arrived." Lady Laetitia's cool blue gaze ran over him, lingering on his limp cravat. "But I'll consider forgiving you for your rudeness if you fetch us three more pineapple ices."

More pineapple? Good Lord, but he was being punished for his sins today. "Of course, my lady. I'll find a waiter—"

"Oh no, that won't do. The waiter is taking an age in this crush, and Lady Caroline, Lady Beatrice and I are dreadfully parched. You'll go yourself, won't you?" She held out her empty silver cup, a sweet smile on her lips, but beneath the brim of her bonnet her eyes were narrowed.

Lady Laetitia was displeased. It was not, alas, an uncommon occurrence.

"I'm delighted to serve you, as always, my lady. Lady Caroline, and Lady Beatrice." He offered them each a bow, then took the sticky cups, loaded them on the tray and made his way across the square, dodging the tangle of carriages, with Hayward smirking after him.

"Lord Windham." One of the waiters darted toward him, his eyes widening when he noticed the tray in Cass's hand. "I beg your pardon, my lord. I didn't see—"

"Never mind, George. I needed the walk." He handed the harried man the tray with a wink. "Three more pineapple ices, and George?"

"Yes, my lord?"

"Take your time."

George grinned. "Yes, my lord."

"Good man."

The tea shop was as crowded inside as it was in the square, the tables teeming with elegant ladies and throngs of their gentlemen admirers lounging about, but he commandeered a coveted space near the door, a bit away from the suffocating press of bodies.

He *was* the Earl of Windham, after all.

A fresh spring breeze scented faintly with lilac reached him where he stood, cooling the perspiration on his forehead and chasing some of the thickest of the cobwebs from his mind. Slowly, his shoulders relaxed, lowering inch by inch until the bottle-green superfine of his collar was no longer touching his earlobes.

Yes, that was better. It would do until he could escape to his townhouse in Mount Street.

He took another deep breath and let the lilac scent wash over him, filling his head and his chest with sweetness. With each breath the tea shop noise faded, and for a moment, just a moment, he let his eyes drop closed and permitted himself to imagine he was somewhere else.

Filtered sunlight, branches swaying over his head, and the soft buzz of dragonfly wings circling a still pond, laughter floating into the blue sky above the tree, and the sweet scent of meadow grasses. It was strange how well he could recall it, strange that the memory never faded in his mind—

"Your pineapple ices, Lord Windham."

The fantasy evaporated in a clatter of dishes and hurried footsteps, and he opened his eyes to find George standing in front of him, a silver tray with three silver dishes atop it balanced on his hand.

"Thank you, George." He took the tray with a sigh and stepped out into Berkeley Square, but he was obliged to wait while a parade of carriages made their way past the door, each one more fashionable than the last, with brass fittings and lacquered paint gleaming in the sunlight.

There was no shortage of fine equipages in Berkeley Square. The *ton* delighted in showing off their elegant taste, and he'd seen similar parades so many times he wouldn't have paid these carriages much attention at all, but at the end of the procession was a *vis-à-vis* phaeton painted a distinctive deep violet color, so dark it was nearly black, with silver-accented wheels and sumptuous pale gray velvet seats.

It was already past him when he noticed it, but he didn't need to see the crest emblazoned on the door to know whose carriage it was. Lady Patience Fosberry, one of the undeniable queens of London society was back in Town, and she'd come out to Berkeley Square today to make certain everyone knew it.

She wasn't alone. Three young ladies were in the carriage with her, the ends of the brightly colored silk ribbons trimming their bonnets fluttering in the breeze. The carriage passed too quickly for him to see their faces, but he did catch a glimpse of golden curls peeking out from under the wide straw brims.

The barouche circled a few times until it found a shady spot on the other side of the square only a few paces away from Lady Laetitia's carriage. He followed in its wake, dodging people and horses as he went and by some miracle holding onto the tray with the melting ices atop it, the sour smell of pineapple making his nose twitch with revulsion.

It was too much. The nauseating scent of the ices, the relentless pounding in his head, Lady Laetitia's imperious commands—he'd had quite enough of it all for one day. He'd deliver the ices to Lady Laetitia and her friends, bid Lady Fosberry a brief welcome to London, as she was one of only a handful of aristocrats who didn't bore him to death, and then he'd take his leave.

But as he neared the knot of carriages on the other side of the square and got a better look at the three young ladies seated in Lady Fosberry's carriage his footsteps slowed, and his heart gave a painful lurch, stealing his breath.

Those young ladies looked just like...

No, surely not. It was impossible.

In all the years they'd been friends, he'd only known her to venture into Town twice. She and her sisters were notoriously averse to the noise and grime of London and preferred to remain at their country estate in Kent.

Yet somehow, impossibly, they were here, not five paces away from him.

Even after all these years, he'd never mistake them.

Margaret and Sarah were on the bench directly behind the driver, their faces animated as they took in the crowd around them. As he watched, Margaret leaned forward and said something to Lady Fosberry. She and the lady next to her turned to glance behind them, and the next thing he knew...

He was gazing into a familiar pair of bluebell-blue eyes.

It had been over a decade since he'd seen her, but as soon as her eyes met his, he knew her at once. There was only one lady in all of England—in all the world, possibly—who had eyes such a deep shade of blue.

Hattie Parrish.

Just like that, a dozen years melted away, and he was back in Kent, lying under the beech tree, the sweet, iced cakes she'd brought in the picnic basket still thick on his tongue, and she was beside him, stringing the lapful of daisies she'd gathered into delicate white and yellow chains.

But this was altogether a different Hattie than the child he remembered. She was no longer the carefree little sprite he recalled, her skirts streaked with dirt and a layer of damp earth under her fingernails.

Of course, she wasn't. Had he imagined time stood still in Kent?

In the twelve years that had passed, she'd blossomed into a young lady. Her wild tangle of fair curls had been tamed into an elegant chignon, and cheeks that had once been ruddy were now pale and smooth, with just the faintest sprinkling of freckles across the bridge of her nose from the kiss of the sun. She was wearing an eye-catching rose-colored gown, the childish, grass-stained pinafores long since laid aside.

She was unspeakably lovely, quite the loveliest lady he'd ever seen.

And all at once, he was unfairly, unaccountably furious.

What was she doing here? She didn't belong here. Not in dirty, crowded London where there was no fresh air to be had, and every breath was tainted with filth. Not here, where the *ton* gossiped and sneered at young ladies from the country behind their backs, and sometimes to their faces.

Not *here*, where scoundrels and fortune-hunters lurked around every corner, just waiting for a sweet, naïve young lady like Hattie Parrish to stumble into their path.

He stalked toward Lady Fosberry's carriage, everything fading to an indistinct blur around him except her face. Her face was all that mattered, all he could see.

The face that lived in his memories and haunted his dreams.

She saw him at once, as if the intensity of his gaze compelled hers. Their eyes met, and a dozen years fell away as if they'd never happened.

The closer he got, the more befuddled she became, her eyes going wide and a pink flush rising in her cheeks. "Cass," she breathed, when he reached the carriage at last. "I—I..."

She trailed off, her cheeks now scarlet, and Lady Fosberry stepped in, offering him a gracious smile. "Lord Windham! My goodness, where did you come from? I had no notion you were in London for the season. How do you do, my lord?"

Cass opened his mouth, but all that emerged was a strangled breath.

Hattie shouldn't be here. He didn't want her here. Not now, after it had taken every bit of strength he possessed to let her letters go unanswered, one after the other, her increasingly frantic pleas for him to write to her tearing at his heart.

Yet here she was, close enough he could touch her, and that...no, that couldn't happen. He'd cut off their friendship because he'd had to, because she was better off without the friendship of the wicked Earl of Windham.

Since he'd left Kent he'd become, every inch of him, his father's son.

"Cassian!" Margaret gave him a tentative smile. "How do you do? It's lovely to see you again after so many years."

49

He didn't reply. He couldn't muster a single word. He could only gaze at Hattie. He wanted to tell her to go, to leave London at once and never return, yet at the same time, the boy he'd once been wanted to beg her to stay.

So, he said nothing, the unspoken words tangling in his throat.

Margaret glanced uneasily at Lady Fosberry when he didn't return her greeting, and once again her ladyship rushed to fill the awkward silence. "Have you brought us some ices, Lord Windham? How very kind of you. I'll summon a waiter, shall I? There are four of us, and only three—"

"What are you doing here?" He wanted to look away from her. It would be easier if he could pretend her eyes weren't as blue as he remembered—cornflowers and blue-bonnets, lobelia and irises with the delicate tracing of white on their deep violet petals.

But it was no use. She was here, and he couldn't tear his gaze from her face.

Her delicate pink lips parted. "Cass? Is that really you? I-I can hardly believe you're standing here. I'm so happy to see you. Did you—"

"You didn't answer my question. What are you doing in London, Lady Harriet?"

FOUR

L ady Harriet.

Hattie stared at him, her heart giving a sickening lurch in her chest, unable to say a single word. In all the time she'd known Cass, he'd never once called her Lady Harriet. To him, she'd always been Hattie.

But she didn't know this man, with his cold dark eyes and grim, unsmiling mouth.

Oh, why had she come here? It had been a mistake, a terrible mistake—

"Windham! Whatever do you mean by keeping these delightful young ladies all to yourself?" The tall, dark-haired man who'd been standing with Cass earlier approached the carriage and offered them a polite bow. "How rude you are! Will you not introduce me?"

For one strained instant, it appeared as if Cass would *not* introduce him. Was he ashamed of them? They weren't as frighteningly elegant as the ladies in the adjacent carriage.

The Cass she remembered would never have been so

openly disdainful of a lady just because she wasn't dressed in the height of fashion, but the man who stood before her now wasn't the Cass she remembered.

This man looked as if he'd stumbled out of *Ackermann's Repository* in his handsome bottle-green superfine cutaway coat, his tight, dark gray pantaloons tucked into a pair of glossy black Hessians, as the latest fashion dictated.

He was tall, his shoulders broad, and the thick waves backlit by the sun were nothing like the tousled, mahogany locks she remembered. His hair was shiny with pomade, the sweet boyish curls cut into a ruthlessly fashionable *coup au vent*.

No, this wasn't Cass. This was the Earl of Windham, and she hadn't the first idea what to say to such an exotic, elegant creature. So, she said nothing, but sat there as silent as a cipher, with her mouth hanging open like a perfect fool.

Thank goodness for Lady Fosberry, who was as adept at smoothing over an awkward situation as any duchess. "Lord Hayward, how do you do? It's been an age, has it not?"

"Since the end of last season, I believe. It's always a great pleasure to see you, my lady. Since Windham's manners seemed to have deserted him, perhaps you'd be good enough to introduce me to your companions."

"Of course, my lord. These young ladies are Lord Melrose's sisters. Lady Margaret, Lady Harriet, and Lady Sarah Parrish, may I present the Earl of Hayward?"

"Melrose's sisters? But how wonderful! Your brother was a faithful friend to my late elder brother James. They attended Oxford together. I accompanied him to a house party at your lovely estate in Kent one summer, although that was years ago now."

"I recall the occasion perfectly." Margaret's cheeks flushed when every head turned toward her in surprise. "I, ah, I mean I vaguely recall meeting one of my brother's companions from Oxford. It was seven years ago, I think."

"Yes, that's right." Lord Hayward offered Margaret a dazzling smile, his handsome dark eyes bright with pleasure. "Now I think of it, I believe we were introduced then, were we not, Lady Margaret?"

"We were, yes, though I'm surprised you remember it, my lord, as I was only fifteen at the time."

"Of course, I do. I remember it with perfect clarity." Lord Hayward bowed over Margaret's hand, his lips hovering chastely over her gloved fingers. "I never forget a face, Lady Margaret."

Margaret's cheeks flushed crimson, and she was looking everywhere but directly at Lord Hayward, which was...a trifle disconcerting, as Margaret wasn't the sort of lady prone to bashful blushes.

"Have you all come to London for the season?" Lord Hayward turned his winning smile on Lady Fosberry. "You are to be commended, my lady, for bringing such charming young ladies to Town."

"They're not here for the season," Cass interrupted in a harsh tone.

Beside her, Sarah let out a soft gasp. It was unforgivably rude for him to answer for them, and Margaret's face darkened to an ominous red, but before either of them could speak Hattie gave a quick shake of her head.

She had no idea what was happening here, but whatever it was it was dreadful, and an argument would only make it worse. She would not engage in a scene in the middle of Berkeley Square with half the *ton* looking on.

"Not here for the season?" Lord Hayward frowned. "How disappointing. But we'll see you at Lady Dumfries's ball at the end of next week, surely? I know what great friends you and Lady Dumfries are, Lady Fosberry."

Lady Fosberry inclined her head. "We'll consider attending, my lord."

"Wonderful. Now then, Windham, the ladies in our party are awaiting their ices, such as they are." Lord Hayward grimaced at the puddles of melted ice in their pewter cups. "I bid you a good day, ladies."

Cass gave them a cool nod, then turned to follow Lord Hayward back to the trio of young ladies waiting in a nearby carriage, all of whom were now staring at them and whispering among themselves.

Hattie watched him go, hot tears pressing against her eyelids.

She wouldn't cry. Dash it, no matter what else happened, she would *not* cry.

"Are we really going to Lady Dumpling's ball?" Sarah clasped her hands and turned her big blue eyes on Lady Fosberry.

"Lady Dumfries, dear, not Dumpling. As to whether we're going or not, I think you'd better address that question to your elder sisters."

"May we, Margaret? Please? Margaret!"

Margaret was miles away, her gaze fixed on Lord Hayward's retreating form, and she jumped at Sarah's exclamation. "For pity's sake, Sarah, what are you shouting about?"

"I asked if we might attend Lady Dumfries's ball. Please? It sounds like ever so much fun, and I've never been to a ball before."

Margaret hesitated. Sarah had never been to a ball or anywhere else, as her fragile health had kept her well out of society until recently. There was nothing that pained Margaret more than disappointing Sarah, but she shook her head. "No, I don't think so, dearest. Our brother wouldn't like it."

Johnathan. Dear God, she'd been so taken up with Cass she'd forgotten all about Johnathan! If he ever found out they'd come here without his approval—without his knowledge, even—he'd be furious with all of them.

Worse, he'd be disappointed in them.

"You let me worry about Johnathan and Emmeline, hmmm?" Lady Fosberry patted Margaret's hand. "If you'd like to attend, my dears, I assure you I can see you safely through a ballroom."

"But what if Johnathan finds out?" Margaret wrung her hands. "He'll be so angry with us, and it will be my fault, as I'm the eldest."

"Now, don't fret, dear." Lady Fosberry waved this away. "If your brother does find out, then we will simply remind him that if it wasn't for the London season, he never would have found Emmeline."

"Yes, indeed! How clever you are, my lady!" Sarah

squealed, clapping her hands together. "If only I'd brought my blue silk gown! It would be just the thing for a ball."

"Not to worry, my dear. We've got gowns in every shade of blue you can imagine here in London. But girls, that was an excessively strange encounter, was it not?" Lady Fosberry glanced back at Cass and Lord Hayward as the carriage slid into the tangle of conveyances then turned the corner at Curzon Street, and they were out of sight. "Even now, I'm still not certain what happened."

"It was decidedly strange, yes. I wouldn't have known Cass." Margaret cast a sidelong glance at Hattie. "He's nothing at all like I remember him."

"It's been years, Margaret." Hattie tried to swallow the lump lodged in her throat. "He's the Earl of Windham now. It's only natural that he's changed."

"The Earl of Windham, indeed, and terribly grand, isn't he?"

"Terribly rude, as well." Sarah sniffed. "He is changed, and not for the better. I don't care if he is a lord now. The way he stared at us! And he was dreadful to Hattie."

Hattie opened her mouth to protest, to find some excuse for Cass, but closed it again without a word. What was there to say? He hadn't merely been rude, he'd been...

Cold.

A shiver wracked her, a spray of goosebumps blooming on her neck despite the warmth of the late afternoon sun. How could the boy she'd loved so well speak to her with such frozen disdain?

"I can't excuse his behavior, but I confess I feel rather sorry for Lord Windham. It couldn't have been easy for him, having to contend with such a father. Hattie, my dear, take this." Lady Fosberry reached for a carriage rug. "You look chilled."

She was chilled, down to her marrow.

"Of course, we've heard the rumors about the previous Earl of Windham, just as everyone else in England has." Margaret tucked the rug around Hattie's knees. "But all we know about him is that Cass appeared in Kent without explanation one summer, and then he was dragged away again three months later. We never knew why."

"Cassian's elder brother died, that's why. Cassian was of no consequence to his father before that, but overnight he became the heir to the title and a substantial fortune."

"His brother?" Hattie turned from the window to stare at Lady Fosberry. "I never heard anything about Cass having a brother."

Why had Cass never confided in her? Never, in all the years they'd been friends, had he breathed a single word of this. Perhaps they hadn't been as close as she'd imagined.

"A half-brother, yes. He was the son of Cassian's father and Lady Diana Ottley, Viscount Ottley's daughter. She died soon after the boy was born, and Cass's father spent the next five years dallying with one lady after another until at last he got a young housemaid in his employ with child. To the *ton*'s shock, he married the girl."

Sarah gasped. "Cass's mother was his father's housemaid?"

"Yes, and you can be certain the *ton* won't ever let him forget it." Lady Fosberry sighed. "It's a rather convoluted story, I'm afraid, and best left for another time."

They lapsed into silence after that as the carriage made its way back to Lady Fosberry's estate in Hampstead Heath, each of them lost in their own thoughts. Sarah was no doubt dreaming of ballrooms and blue silk gowns, and Margaret was perhaps reliving the moment when handsome Lord Hayward had bowed over her hand.

Hattie rubbed her hands together to warm them.

She wouldn't cry. She *wouldn't...*

But despite her best efforts, by the time they reached the front door hot, stinging tears were pressing against her eyelids.

She'd dreamed a thousand dreams about the moment she and Cass would meet again, and in the time it took to drive from Berkeley Square to Hampstead Heath all her girlish fancies had crumbled to dust.

Very well, then. She *would* cry, but she'd do it in the privacy of her own bedchamber. As soon as they were inside, she went directly to the staircase, but before she could make her escape, Lady Fosberry stopped her.

"A word in the drawing room, if you'd be so kind, Harriet."

There was no kindness to be found inside her, only confusion and heartache. How could she have been so foolish as to think Cass would be pleased to see her? Never, in all the years they'd been friends, had he ever treated her so dismissively as he had this afternoon.

The look in his eyes, the coldness there—

"Hattie, Lady Fosberry is speaking to you." Margaret had reached the first-floor landing, but she paused and glanced over her shoulder, her worried blue gaze pausing on Hattie.

"Go on. I'll check on Sarah while you have a chat with Lady Fosberry."

It seemed there was to be a chat, whether she wished it or not. Silently, she followed Lady Fosberry down the corridor to the drawing room, her feet dragging with every step.

"Sit down, dear." Lady Fosberry waved a hand at the yellow silk settee. "Tea?"

"No, thank you, my lady." The sooner this discussion was over the better, because it felt as if a lead ball was lodged in her stomach, and she wasn't at all sure she wouldn't cast up her accounts all over Lady Fosberry's pretty, silk settee.

"Very well." Lady Fosberry settled herself comfortably among the pillows before turning the direct gaze that was the scourge of the upper ten thousand on Hattie. "That meeting with Lord Windham was a bit awkward, was it not?"

Awkward? My, that was an optimistic interpretation.

Hattie let out a hollow laugh. "It was a good deal more than awkward, my lady. Lord Windham came as close to giving me the cut direct as I've ever seen."

How had it come to this? It was one thing for Cass to break off their correspondence. It wasn't proper, after all, for a single gentleman to write to a lady he was not betrothed to. At least, that was how she'd excused Cass's sudden silence to herself.

But she knew better, now. The way he'd glared at her with those ice-cold eyes, it was as if he'd never seen her before, as if they'd never been friends.

Devastating would be a more appropriate word. Heart-breaking.

Lady Fosberry considered this and shook her head. "I don't deny Lord Windham was startled to see you here in London, my dear, but I wouldn't call it a cut direct."

What did it matter what they called it? "I think...I think I've made a mistake coming here, my lady."

She didn't belong here. That had become painfully obvious after one glance at the fashionable young ladies in Cass's party this afternoon. She wasn't elegant or witty, and she didn't know a thing about fashion.

Was it any wonder he'd stopped writing to her? He must have found her quaint account of her quiet life unbearably dull. Why, in her last letter to him she'd given a detailed description of the bluebells blossoming in the filtered sunlight of the oak grove behind the stables! She'd even drawn a picture of them.

It made her cringe to think of that letter now. How provincial he must find her!

If nothing else, this afternoon's debacle had confirmed what she'd always suspected.

The best place for her was in her quiet little corner of Kent, mucking about in her gardens in her dusty boots and breathing the fresh country air. "I think it's best if I return to Kent at once, my lady. I beg your pardon for causing you so much trouble."

Lady Fosberry said nothing, only gazed at her, her expression giving nothing away.

Hattie squirmed under that direct gaze, but surely Lady Fosberry must see that her remaining in London was utterly out of the question. Just the idea of it made her stomach lurch with panic.

"My sisters may stay, if they like. There's no reason for either of them to return to—"

"Why did you come to London, Hattie?"

It was a simple enough question, but she found herself floundering for an answer. "Because he...because I...the scandal sheets...I thought perhaps I could help Cass."

Now she'd said it aloud, it struck her as an absurd reason to come scurrying to London. *She*, help *him*? He was an earl, for pity's sake!

"I see. And you've changed your mind after one afternoon? You no longer wish to help Cass?"

"No! No, of course I do, but—"

"My dear girl, I thought Cassian's friendship meant more to you than that."

"He...I..."

Dash it, here came the tears she'd tried so valiantly to suppress, spilling from her eyes and down her cheeks, her nose burning with them. "His friendship means a great deal to me, my lady." It meant everything, but it wasn't as if she could remain friends with Cass against his will. "But he doesn't appear to feel the same way."

Lady Fosberry's expression softened. "On the contrary, Hattie. He felt a great deal."

"I don't know why you think so." Hattie plucked at her skirts, avoiding Lady Fosberry's eyes. "He hardly spared me a glance."

"I don't deny it. He deliberately avoided looking at you."

Well, that was plain enough. Just like that, any lingering

hope that she'd somehow misread Cass's reaction evaporated in a puff of smoke. "He made his sentiments regarding our friendship quite clear."

"My dearest girl!" Lady Fosberry laid a hand over hers, stilling her restless fingers. "A gentleman does not make such a point of not meeting the eyes of a lady for whom he feels nothing."

"I'm sorry, my lady, but I still think it's best if I leave."

"Very well, Hattie, if you insist upon it, then I'll send you back to Kent tomorrow in my coach. But first, I wish to tell you something."

Dear God, what now? But she could hardly refuse. "Yes, of course."

"I warn you it's not a happy tale." Lady Fosberry drew in a deep breath. "By all accounts the Earl of Windham's first son was a sickly child. The earl was in constant terrors he'd expire, so when he got his housemaid with child, he married the girl to ensure his second son could inherit the earldom, if it came to it."

"How dreadful. He sounds quite calculating."

"He was, indeed. The previous earl was a man of neither warmth nor decency. He married the girl, then promptly abandoned her and her son. Despite the marriage, Cassian and his mother never lived with him. He paid them no mind at all until his elder son's health took a dangerous turn. Cassian's mother was dead by then."

"That must have been when Cass came to Kent." It was all falling into place now. Cass's deep resentment when he arrived, and his bitterness toward his father.

"Yes. The earl plucked him out of St. Giles and sent him

to his old friend Lord Balfour in Chatham. Balfour was meant to keep an eye on him until Cass's half-brother either recovered or died."

"And he died." The child had died, and Cass's fate was sealed.

"The lad held on for a few months, but yes, he eventually succumbed, the poor thing. Cassian became the heir, and I can assure you, my dear, being the Earl of Windham's heir was no easy task. Cassian was still quite young when he was turned over to his father's care. It must have been confusing for him, and I dare say his father has since filled his head with poison."

"How terrible." Was it any wonder Cass was no longer the sweet, affectionate boy he'd once been?

"I don't know Cassian well," Lady Fosberry went on, "But there is some indication he's following in his father's footsteps. There has been some, ah, unfortunate behavior—"

"The wagering, drinking and brawling, you mean. Yes, Alice Weatherby wrote Sarah all about it. According to Alice, Cass is as wicked an earl as London has ever seen."

"Perhaps, but I haven't yet given up on Cassian. Lord Hayward is a good soul, and he's loyal to his friend. If Cassian were beyond hope, Lord Hayward would long since have washed his hands of him. Still, I daresay Lord Windham could use as many true friends as he can find."

Lady Fosberry spoke carefully, her tone neutral, but the words echoed deep inside Hattie nonetheless, like a bell that continues to ring long after it's struck.

And after all, wasn't part of this merely her wounded pride?

She had hoped Cass would be thrilled to see her, that he'd welcome her with open arms. But he hadn't, and here she was, ready to scurry back to her safe little nook in the country.

After more than a decade of friendship, would she give up on Cass so easily?

Lady Fosberry was right. That wasn't what a true friend would do.

It was what a coward would do.

"My dearest Hattie, I don't say this to make you ashamed of yourself, so please do endeavor not to look quite so stricken, would you?"

She dashed a hand across her cheek and produced a watery smile for Lady Fosberry. "I beg your pardon, my lady."

"Nonsense, my dear." Lady Fosberry patted her hand. "I do understand your reticence, you know. It's quite a task you've undertaken, but you've come this far, and I think you'll be disappointed in yourself if you give up so easily."

She was interrupted by a quiet knock on the door, and a moment later Watkins, Lady Fosberry's butler came in. "This came for you, my lady."

"Thank you, Watkins." Lady Fosberry scanned the thick, cream-colored card. "Ah, it seems the *ton* knows I've returned to Town. Word does travel quickly, does it not? Lady Farthingale has invited us to her garden party tomorrow morning."

"A garden party?" That didn't sound too terrifying.

"Yes. Lady Farthingale's garden party is one of the most coveted invitations of the season. She's famous for her lilacs, you see, and there's a lovely lilac walk on the grounds of her estate. It's a tradition for each gentleman to invite a lady to stroll amongst the lilacs with him." Lady Fosberry raised an eyebrow. "Shall I accept for the four of us, or just for myself and your sisters?"

"I suppose it won't hurt to remain for another few days, if you think it will help Cass."

After that cold, dismissive look he'd given her, she didn't have much hope her presence would make any difference to him, but if she stayed, then she wouldn't have to reproach herself for being such a coward.

"I do think so. Indeed, I think..." Lady Fosberry's smile dimmed. "I think you may be the only person in England who can help Cass now."

CHAPTER

FIVE

This was a disaster. An utter and complete disaster.

Hayward had unwittingly unleashed a nest of hornets with his innocent suggestion that Lady Fosberry and her charges attend next week's ball. It might start with Lady Dumfries, but it wouldn't end there. Next it would be the promenade, then Gunter's for pineapple ices, then the theater, and the next he knew, Hattie would be waltzing at Almack's.

They'd be in it then, and once that happened, there would be no going back. If the Parrish sisters ventured into society, there would be no chance of them ever returning to obscurity again. The *ton* would sink their claws into them, and when they had them, they wouldn't easily relinquish them.

Every despicable fortune-hunting scoundrel in London would be after their dowries, and the Parrish sisters no better off than lambs awaiting the slaughter.

He had to see Hattie, now. It was well past calling hours, but it couldn't be helped.

"What the devil is the matter with you now, Windham? Is it the pineapple ices again?" Hayward cast a baffled look at him as they made their way back to Lady Laetitia's carriage. "You were unforgivably rude to Melrose's sisters, and you look as if you've seen a ghost."

Hayward had no idea how right he was. "I haven't got time to explain myself now. Make my excuses to Lady Laetitia, would you?"

"Make your...what are you on about, Windham? Where are you going? You can't simply abandon Lady Laetitia without a word of—"

"Forgive me, Hayward." Cass pushed the tray with the melting ices into Hayward's startled hands. "But I must go at once. I've an urgent matter to attend to."

"Is this about Melrose's sisters?" Hayward clutched the edges of the tray. The ice cups slid across the slick surface and the melted cream spilled in a sticky rivulet over the edges of the cups. "Please tell me you're not following them to Lady Fosberry's."

Cass said nothing, but Hayward knew him too well to be fooled.

"For God's sake, Windham, have you lost your wits? It's far too late to pay a call now! You can't descend on Lady Fosberry so late in the day. It's not done. Wait until tomorrow, and I'll accompany you to—"

"No. I beg your pardon, Hayward, but this can't wait." Lady Dumfries's ball was in less than a week, and in any case, what he had to say to Hattie was best said in private. "You'll offer my excuses to Lady Laetitia?"

Hayward hesitated, but at last he gave a reluctant nod. "I don't see that I have much choice, but—"

"Good man, Hayward." Cass gave his friend a grateful thump on the back and turned to go, but Hayward's voice stopped him.

"A moment, Windham. I'll make your excuses, but I'll be awaiting a full explanation for your odd behavior."

"You'll get one. I promise it." He owed Hayward that much, but not a single soul in London could ever find out the entire truth.

Not even Hattie. Especially not Hattie.

It seemed to take a lifetime for him to ride from Berkeley Square to Hampstead Heath. By the time he arrived the shadows were lengthening across the rolling green lawns and the formal gardens of Lady Fosberry's estate.

How was he going to explain his presence here at this time of day? Lady Fosberry was hardly the stickler for propriety that so many others in London were, but neither was she likely to be pleased to find him on her doorstep at such an hour.

But as he dismounted and made his way toward the door, a flash of movement in the garden to the right of the house caught his eye. It looked like...the flutter of a lady's skirt hems moving across one of the graveled garden pathways.

A rose-colored skirt hem, if he wasn't mistaken.

Here was some luck, at last!

"Wait here, Sampson." He ran his palm down his horse's

silky nose, then looped his reins around one of the iron posts surrounding the rose garden. "I won't be long. There's a good boy."

By the time he turned around Hattie had vanished, having melted into the darkness, but he'd find her.

He stepped onto the pathway, his boots crunching quietly against the stones, and passed into the garden.

THE PROBLEM with London was that it was impossible to find space to breathe.

At least, that was one of the problems. The dust and dirt, the noise and crowds of people, the streets choked with carriages and carts and littered with horse droppings were terribly unpleasant as well, but it was the lack of open space that truly appalled her.

Hattie paused at the corner of the small garden laid out on the east edge of Lady Fosberry's lawn. It was a pretty spot, beautifully tended and large by London's standards, but it was cramped indeed when compared to the Kentish countryside.

Here, one could hardly move a dozen paces before encountering the elegant iron fencing that separated it from the formal rose gardens on either side of it.

How she longed for the bright open meadows that surrounded Melrose House in Kent! She'd be home soon enough—as soon as she possibly could be—but until then she'd make what she could of this garden and be thankful that Lady Fosberry didn't live in Berkeley Square.

She marched to the opposite corner of the garden, then back again in the other direction—back and forth, back and forth, her mind whirling with questions that had no answers.

They were to attend Lady Farthingale's garden party tomorrow morning. Would she see Cass there? If so, how was she meant to behave towards him? What was she meant to say? Whatever else happened she must be careful not to attract the attention of the gossiping *ton*. If there was even a whisper of scandal attached to them, Johnathan might hear of it, and goodness knew what would happen then. He was a mild-tempered man, but he was terribly protective of them, and he wouldn't easily overlook a secret jaunt to London.

And it might have all been for nothing—

"You never did answer my question this afternoon, Lady Harriet."

She'd paced to the opposite corner of the garden again, but she turned at the rumble of that deep voice, and her feet froze in place.

It was past seven o'clock in the evening, and the sun was just sinking below the horizon, washing everything around them in shades of gold and orange. She couldn't quite make out his face at this distance, but there was no mistaking that voice.

It was him. Of course, it was him.

His voice had deepened since she'd heard it last, yet she knew every vibration of it, every chord and texture as if it were a beloved song she'd played so often each note of it was etched in her memory.

It was as familiar to her as the beat of her own heart.

She'd heard him tease, she'd heard him lecture, she'd heard his whisper in her ear, low and confiding, and she'd heard that voice light with laughter, but never—not once—had she ever heard it as cold as it was now.

It was his voice, and not his at the same time.

She'd hardly recognized Cass when she saw him earlier today. The man he'd become wasn't at all like the boy he'd once been. His father had been a Corinthian and a Whip, and despite his wickedness, a fashionable man about town. He was accepted by the *ton* and welcomed everywhere he went.

But he'd been cold down to the deepest depths of his black heart.

It would be easy to believe that was the sort of man Cass had become. Grand and fashionable, but underneath his handsome face and elegant trimmings, callous and debauched.

But the loneliness she'd sensed in him when he first came to Kent all those years ago clung to him still, despite his aristocratic friends. Anyone who didn't know him well wouldn't have noticed it, but now he was so close to her, she could see it.

She could see *him*. Everything he was, and everything he tried to hide.

It was as plain to her as lines written in a book.

She raised her chin and sucked in a breath to clear the tremble from her throat.

"What are you doing here, Cass?"

Had he come to beg her pardon for his coldness earlier? Hope rose in her breast, even as she cursed herself for a fool.

Yet it would not be contained, pressing with wild abandon against her rib cage.

There was something so familiar about him, standing under the cherry tree that dominated the center of the garden, its slender dark branches now laden with thick clusters of pink flowers.

For as long as she'd known him, flowers and Cass had always gone together. Unbidden, a memory rose in her mind of him bent over a pile of daisies in his lap, his tongue resting in the corner of his mouth as he concentrated on stringing the delicate blooms together into a chain.

His hands were too big to make quick work of it, even then. She glanced at his hands hanging loosely by his sides and a strange sensation passed over her, settling in her lower belly.

"I told you already." He stepped closer, a shadow with broad shoulders that blocked the last dim rays of sunlight. "I've come for an answer to my question. Have you come to London for the season, my lady?"

Ah, it was still my lady, was it? He'd chased her all the way here from Berkeley Square, but even so, he insisted on keeping this distance between them.

Her heart, ridiculous organ that it was, sank into the pit of her stomach. "Does Lady Fosberry know you've sneaked into her garden?"

"No. This has nothing to do with Lady Fosberry, or anyone else. This is between us."

He took another step, then another until he was close enough she might have reached out a touched him.

She didn't. But neither did she retreat. She'd made a

promise to Lady Fosberry, and she wouldn't break it. "The London Horticultural Society is having a lecture series next week. Are you aware of that, my lord?"

"The London Horticultural Society," he repeated flatly. "You've come all the way from Kent to hear a lecture?"

"Not *a* lecture, but a series of lectures. Sir Joseph Banks is meant to speak on his improvements to Kew Gardens. I daresay it will be fascinating."

It took everything in her not to squirm as he scrutinized her face. She'd never lied to Cass before, and already she could feel a guilty flush heating her cheeks.

"You're a dreadful liar, Lady Harriet. Now, have you, or have you not come for the season? You seem reluctant to answer my question. I wonder why that is?"

"Perhaps it's because you have no right to ask it. My plans are no concern of yours, Lord Windham."

He flinched slightly at her use of his title, and a surge of satisfaction swept through her, only to dissipate at once in a hot rush of shame. Since when had she ever taken pleasure in hurting Cass? "As I told you, we've come to London to hear the London Horti—"

"And as I told you, I believe you're lying. If you have come for the season, I advise you to return to Kent at once. I insist upon it."

She stared at him. What was happening right now? Was Cass truly standing here in front of her after all this time, his dark eyes as cold as stone, ordering her to leave London? "I don't understand. Why should we—"

"The sooner you take your leave, the better. Preferably

before Lady Dumfries's ball next week. A *ton* ballroom is no place for naïve young ladies from the country."

She wasn't quick-tempered, but at his dismissive tone the first pangs of anger began to stir in her breast, and she raised her chin. "Are you ordering me out of London, Cass?"

Something flashed across his face then—hesitation, or shame, perhaps—but it was gone so quickly she couldn't be certain, and then he straightened his shoulders and met her eyes. "Yes. You shouldn't be here. You're not fit for a London season, Lady Harriet."

Not fit! Was he saying she wasn't worthy of a season? Why, how dare he? That she *hadn't* come for the season—and indeed, there were very few things less appealing to her than a London season—utterly slipped her mind in that moment.

"Have you forgotten that the Earl of Melrose is my brother? I'm the sister of a respectable earl, Lord Windham. The season was invented for aristocratic young ladies just like me."

He was unnaturally still, his shoulders rigid. "For aristocratic young ladies, yes, but not for *you*, Lady Harriet. You haven't the first idea how to manage the *ton* under the best of circumstances, much less during a season."

It was true. There were dozens of rules young ladies were meant to follow during the season—hundreds of them—and she hadn't the first idea about any of them. Johnathan and Emmeline didn't care for London or the *ton* and assiduously avoided the season.

The cowardly part of her that always seemed to be lying in wait came lurching to the fore, and for a shameful moment she wanted more than anything to fly back to Kent and leave London far behind.

But she would not be bullied, not even by Cass.

She straightened her shoulders. "Lady Fosberry thinks otherwise. So, while I thank you for your concern, Lord Windham, where I choose to spend my time is no concern of yours."

"Do you have any idea what sort of scoundrels come to London for the season, Lady Harriet? The worst sort of fortune-hunters, gamblers and rakehells. Do you suppose you can tell the difference between a gentleman and a rogue? I think not."

Did he think her an utter simpleton? It was true she hadn't spent much time away from Kent, but she wasn't so dimwitted she couldn't tell the difference between a villain and a proper gentleman.

Anger swelled inside her, sudden and searing, and before she could think better of it her mouth was opening, and words were tumbling from her lips.

No, not just words. *Lies.*

"I'm sorry you think so, my lord, but we're here now, and we have indeed come for the season."

God above, those were not words she'd ever imagined would fall from her lips, but they were out there now, and there was no taking them back. Even if she could, she wouldn't. Cass—that is, Lord Windham—had no business ordering her about.

She'd do as she pleased, just as she'd told him she would. Not that a season was at all likely to please her, but the thing was as good as done, now.

Cass's hands clenched. "You're making a mistake, Lady Harriet. You have no idea what you're getting yourself—"

"As I said, my lord, I thank you for your opinion, but I will do as I please. Lady Fosberry has agreed to sponsor us, and we'll be attending Lady Farthingale's garden party tomorrow morning."

He took another step toward her, his long shadow swallowing her, and to her everlasting humiliation, she took a small step backwards. Dear God, but he seemed utterly gigantic here in this diminutive garden.

"Is that so? I'll just have a word with your brother about it first, shall I, my lady?"

Oh, no. No, no, no.

If Cass discovered she and her sisters had come to London without Johnathan and Emmeline—without their approval or even their knowledge—this ruse would be over before it could even begin. They'd be packed off to Kent so quickly their heads would spin.

What was she to do? There was only one answer.

Lie. *Again.*

"I'm afraid that won't be possible. At least, not tonight. Even if it weren't well past calling hours—and it is—my brother and Lady Melrose won't arrive in London until tomorrow afternoon."

"Tomorrow," he repeated flatly. The dark eyes she remembered so well narrowed, but he couldn't possibly know she was lying.

Could he?

"Yes. They were unexpectedly detained in Kent and are a day or so behind us."

"You'll do me the courtesy, my lady, of letting your brother and Lady Melrose know that I intend to call on them tomorrow."

"Oh, I'm afraid that won't do. You see, we don't expect them until well past calling hours, my lord." It was a desperate enough ploy and would only gain her another day at the most, but she'd already told half a dozen lies by now. What was one more?

"Tomorrow evening, then."

"No, that won't do, either, as they're sure to be fatigued after their journey."

He raised an eyebrow. "Fatigued by a drive from Kent to London? It doesn't take more than half a day to make that drive, Lady Harriet. Unless Lord Melrose is a great deal more enfeebled than I recall, I find it difficult to believe he won't have the strength for a brief meeting."

Of course, he did, because it was a bald-faced lie, and she was digging herself deeper with every word out of her mouth, but she'd gone too far to give up the truth now.

"You may believe what you like, my lord, but it doesn't change the fact that my brother and Lady Melrose will not be at home to visitors tomorrow evening."

Or anytime. Not to Lord Windham.

He didn't reply, but gazed down at her with an expression that would have flayed the skin from the bones of a lesser woman. He'd been in London for less than a year, but in that time, he'd perfected the withering aristocratic stare.

"Very well, Lady Harriet," he said at last. "I'll return the day after tomorrow to call on Lord and Lady Melrose. You'll let them know to expect me?"

"Of course, my lord."

"Then I will bid you a good evening." He offered her a coldly formal bow. "I will see you at Lady Farthingale's garden party tomorrow."

She remained where she was until he was gone, gazing at the spot under the cherry tree where Cass had been standing only moments before, every inch of her trembling as the clop of his horse's hooves on the drive faded to silence.

When he was gone at last her shoulders sagged, and she collapsed onto a nearby stone bench, her legs shaking.

Dear God, what had she just done? She must have gone temporarily mad to commit herself and her sisters to a London season! For pity's sake, Johnathan and Emmeline didn't even know they were here, and now they were about to embark on an endless whirl of social engagements, without her brother's permission?

And that was saying nothing of the lies she'd told. She'd lied to Johnathan by omission, she'd lied to Cass about Johnathan, and worse, she'd embroiled her sisters and Lady Fosberry in her lie about the season.

God above, what had she been thinking?

She *hadn't* been, that was plain, but Cass had been so dismissive, so certain she couldn't hold her own among the *ton* that she'd lost her mind for a moment.

Or perhaps not.

If she was going to help Cass, she must be in his company. That was by no means a simple matter, as there was little opportunity for a gently bred young lady to find herself in the company of a wicked earl. Without the season to bring them together months could pass without her ever laying eyes on him.

But the season offered unique opportunities in that regard. He'd already said he'd see her at Lady Farthingale's party tomorrow.

It was a start, at least. Perhaps tomorrow she'd get a chance to tell him...

To tell him...

Very well, so this part was a little fuzzy in her mind, but she'd think of something.

She had to.

Because Cass was still her dearest friend, regardless of whether he returned her warm sentiments. She'd never forgive herself if she stood by and allowed him to destroy himself without lifting a finger to stop it.

CHAPTER

SIX

"Garden parties are awful things, Windham." Hayward drained the last of his lemonade and set the tiny glass cup aside. "I will bear you a grudge for all eternity for dragging me here today."

"You're in a temper." To be fair, he had forced his friend from his bed rather early this morning, and after a late night at White's last evening, too. Poor Hayward, who made it a point to be impeccably attired, was a trifle less splendid than usual today.

And that was putting it kindly. To put it unkindly, he looked as if he'd been dragged backward through a knothole.

"You may blame Lady Farthingale for my temper," Hayward shot back with a scowl. "Of all the dull entertainments with which the *ton* contrives to amuse themselves during the season, the garden party is the most diabolical."

"Diabolical? That's doing it a bit brown, surely. What's so diabolical about them? It seems a pleasant enough way to pass a morning."

"That's the treachery of the thing! Don't you see, Windham? They seduce one with promises of sun and fresh air. Who, after all, can complain of sunshine and fresh air?"

"You seem to be doing a good job of it, Hayward."

"Nonsense. I never complain."

Cass snorted. "No, of course not."

"It's the stinging insects I take issue with, and the unpredictability of the weather. It's London in the spring, for God's sake. And would you look at poor old Lady Everhardt stumbling about? The uneven ground is a hazard for the less sure-footed among us. Mark my words, Windham. Today will end with a half-dozen twisted ankles."

Cass nodded, but he was only half-listening to this harangue. His attention was on Lady Laetitia, who was arranging herself to picturesque advantage on a picnic blanket in the center of Lady Farthingale's lawn.

"Dear God, I'm parched." Hayward fumbled for his handkerchief and patted the perspiration from his brow. "Why is it so bloody hot? And what does Lady Farthingale mean, serving lemonade in a glass the size of a thimble?"

Cass shrugged. He didn't have the patience for Hayward's theatrics. He needed his wits about him this morning, just in case Hattie did come today, as she'd vowed she would.

The stubborn chit.

Someone had to keep an eye on the Parrish sisters until Lord Melrose arrived in London. Lady Fosberry would do her part, yes, but she couldn't watch all three of them at once, and it wasn't as if they'd go unnoticed. With their pretty faces and fat dowries, every scoundrel in London would be upon them like insects buzzing around a tray of sweets.

God knew no one else in London was going to keep them out of mischief, aside from Lady Fosberry, so for better or worse, the task had fallen on him. Yet at the same time it couldn't appear as if he were preoccupied with them, unless he wished to bring Lady Laetitia's ire down upon them.

A tricky balance, that, and he'd made a mess of it yesterday.

It had been careless of him to linger beside Lady Fosberry's carriage in Berkeley Square. Laetitia had taken notice of it. She hadn't been at all pleased about it, and her mother, Lady Tremblay would be apoplectic if she suspected he'd slighted Laetitia in favor of the Parrish sisters.

Some ten paces away, Laetitia had settled at last, and a knot of young ladies were now gathered around her, fluttering about like a kaleidoscope of pastel butterflies. Yes, that would do. Laetitia wasn't likely to move if she remained at the center of a crowd of admirers.

But perhaps Hattie wouldn't come, after all, despite her threats yesterday. She hadn't made an appearance yet, and the party had begun nearly an hour ago.

She'd never made a secret of her distaste for Town and the *ton*. No, of course she wouldn't come—

"Well, well, well." Beside him, Hayward let out a low whistle. "What have we here?"

Cass turned to follow the direction of Hayward's gaze and froze. There, standing in the open French doors that led out onto Lady Farthingale's terrace stood Margaret, Hattie and Sarah Parrish, with every eye upon them.

It shouldn't have surprised him that Hattie had proved to be as good as her word. She'd warned him she'd certainly be here this morning, but still he stood there gaping at her like a fool as she stepped onto the edge of the lawn, the morning sun flirting with the bright golden strands of her hair.

Margaret followed her, then Lady Fosberry, nodding at something Lady Dumfries was saying to her, her arm linked with Sarah's.

But it was Hattie he couldn't look away from.

She turned toward him, as if she could feel the weight of his gaze on her. Their eyes met, and just like that they were opposite poles circling each other, the attraction holding them in its thrall even when there were dozens of people between them.

"Do stop gawking, Windham. You're gaping at them as if you've seen an apparition. Then again, one can hardly blame you. The Parrish sisters are rather decorative, are they not? I'll say this for garden parties. The young ladies do appear to great advantage in the sunshine. They're rather like exotic birds, with their bright skirts and parasols."

Cass merely grunted, but Hayward wasn't deterred. "Tell me, which of the Parrish sisters has taken your fancy?"

"None of them," Cass lied, turning away. "I don't know what you're talking about. I don't have any interest in any of them."

"Of course, you do. You're a dreadful liar, Windham. There isn't a man alive who wouldn't notice the Parrish sisters. I'm rather partial to Sarah Parrish, myself. Odd, really, as I don't recall her being a particularly promising child when I visited Melrose in Kent, but she was quite young at the time." Hayward cocked his head, studying her. "Lovely girl, and a bit saucy, I think. I do like a lady of spirit."

"She was sickly as a child and was kept mostly indoors, apart from any excitement." Hattie had confided in one of her letters that for years the family had lived in fear they'd lose Sarah. "She suffered from weak lungs."

Hayward's eyebrows shot up. "Indeed? She appears perfectly sturdy now. But tell me, how do you happen to know so much about the Parrish family?"

Damn it. "I don't…I never said I…I suppose I must have heard it somewhere."

"I see. Is that all? Because you behaved rather oddly when we met them at Gunter's yesterday. No one would ever accuse you of being charming, Windham, but I've never known your manners to fail so thoroughly as they did yesterday."

He couldn't deny it. He'd behaved abominably, and one could never get away with ungentlemanly behavior around Hayward. "I didn't—"

"Never mind, Windham." Hayward waved a hand. "Keep your secrets, if you must."

Just then, Sarah threw her head back in a tinkling laugh at something Lady Fosberry had said, and several people turned to smile at her as the sweet sound echoed in the clear morning air.

"Nothing wrong with her lungs now," Hayward remarked. "Very pretty, indeed. Perhaps I'll invite her to accompany me on the lilac walk. Shall we go and greet them?"

It wasn't a good idea. God only knew what he'd blurt out

as soon as he opened his mouth. He'd learned to be careful with people once he'd inherited his title, but he had no defenses against Hattie.

How could he? She knew him too well for that, better even than he knew himself.

"Not me, thank you." Lady Laetitia had been staring at him since the Parrish sisters arrived, her chilly blue gaze like an artic blast against the side of his face. "You go on, Hayward."

He nudged Hayward toward the bright little trio then turned his back on them, instead making his way across the lawn toward Laetitia, but he couldn't banish Hattie from his mind as easily as he banished her from his sight.

What was she *doing* here? He'd asked her a dozen times yesterday, but she'd never given him a satisfactory answer to that question. She claimed they'd come for the Horticultural Society's lectures, to hear Sir Joseph Banks, but as interested as Hattie was in plants and flowers, the lectures were hardly enough to lure her to London.

Especially during the season.

What could possibly have induced her to come here, then? And where the devil were Lord and Lady Melrose? Had their brother truly sent his sisters to London unaccompanied, as Hattie claimed?

It didn't seem likely. Johnathan Parrish was wildly protective of his younger sisters, yet here they were, at the mercy of every fortune hunter and scoundrel in Town for the season, and Melrose nowhere to be found.

Damn it, none of this made any sense.

If Hattie intended to remain for the entirety of the

season, he was certain to encounter her at every social event the *haute ton* had to offer. Lord Melrose was a well-respected gentleman, admired by all. No one would dream of offending him by slighting his sisters, and they were Lady Fosberry's guests, as well. Her ladyship knew everyone and was invited everywhere.

"Windham, here you are at last." Lady Tremblay, Laetitia's mother laid a proprietary hand on his arm as he joined their company. "Not a moment too soon, too. We're panting for some lemonade, aren't we, Laetitia?"

Laetitia didn't reply, nor did she offer him so much as a good morning, but nodded toward the Parrish sisters, her blue eyes narrowed. "Aren't those the same ladies we saw at Gunter's yesterday?"

Cass ignored the question, offering her a bow instead. "Good morning, Laetitia. Will you have lemonade or tea?"

But Laetitia would not be put off so easily. "Yes, I'm sure that's them. How curious, that they should have turned up again. I never laid eyes on them before yesterday. Who are they, Windham?"

"Nobody, by the looks of them." Lady Tremblay gave a disdainful sniff. "My dear Laetitia, their gowns! They have a whiff of the country about them. Why, they look as if they've just stumbled into London from some tragically dusty corner of Cumbria, or some other similarly dreadful place."

"They're with Lady Fosberry, mamma. They must be *somebody*. Windham?" Laetitia's tone was courteous enough, but a layer of ice lurked underneath her practiced charm.

There would be no keeping this secret. If he didn't tell

them, someone else would. "Lady Margaret, Hat—er, Lady Harriet, and Lady Sarah Parrish. They're Lord—"

"Lord Melrose's sisters," Laetitia finished with a sidelong glance at her mother. "Yes, I remember Lord Melrose. He was the nonesuch some decade or so ago, I believe. But how wonderful the Parrish family has found their way back to London! Isn't it wonderful, mamma?"

Lady Tremblay did not appear to find it wonderful at all. If her glower had had the power to set fire, the Parrish sisters would promptly have burst into flames. "I don't see Lord Melrose anywhere about."

"No. I don't believe the earl and Lady Melrose have arrived in London yet."

"What, you mean they sent the three sisters here *alone?*" Lady Tremblay gave him a scandalized look. "How excessively peculiar."

He'd just been thinking the same thing, but he'd be damned if he'd agree with Lady Tremblay. "I don't see why. Lady Fosberry appears to have them well in hand."

"Yes, well, Lady Fosberry does enjoy her misfits, does she not? You will cease staring at them at once, Laetitia," Lady Tremblay snapped, turning her back on them. "The Parrish sisters are nothing to us."

If that were truly the case, he might have rested easier, but precisely what he'd hoped wouldn't happen was now happening. Hattie, Margaret and Sarah had caught the attention of the Tremblay family, and God knew that was sure to cause no end of trouble.

This was what came of Melrose's absence, damn the man. Even Lady Tremblay wouldn't dare to make a move against the Earl of Melrose—he was too wealthy and too well-connected for that, but the presence of the sisters alone in London could well prove too tempting for Lady Tremblay to resist, even if it meant tangling with Lady Fosberry.

"Do fetch us some lemonade, won't you, Windham? Come, Laetitia. Lady Peregrine is just over there, and we haven't yet bid her a good morning."

Laetitia didn't move. She was still watching the Parrish sisters, and there was no mistaking the calculating look in her eyes. It didn't bode well, that look. He'd seen it often enough to know that.

"Lord Egerton appears to have taken a fancy to them." Laetitia nodded toward the terrace, a knowing little smirk on her lips.

Egerton! Despite his efforts not to give himself away, Cass's head jerked toward the terrace so violently his neck cracked.

Of all the scoundrels that haunted London's streets, Egerton was the very worst of the lot. No one would ever guess it to look at him, but underneath his handsome face and celebrated charm, the title and the impeccable clothing the man was devious, malicious, and as slippery as a snake.

"You look troubled, Lord Windham, and I can't imagine why." Lady Laetitia turned to him, that strange smirk still on her lips. "Isn't Lord Egerton a friend of yours?"

He had been, once, but that was before he'd discovered whom—and what—Egerton was.

"He intends to marry this year, you know," Laetitia went on. "I daresay any one of the Parrish sisters could do far worse than to become Lady Egerton."

"For pity's sake, Laetitia," Lady Tremblay snapped. "I haven't the faintest interest in Lord Melrose's sisters' marriage prospects. Now, come at once, will you? Lady Peregrine awaits."

Lady Tremblay moved off in Lady Peregrine's direction with Laetitia following her, and he went off to fetch their blasted lemonade, which took far longer than it should have done, as it was an unusually warm morning, and the entire party wanted lemonade.

He did his best not to stare at Hattie, but everywhere he looked, every time he turned his head she was there, either in his direct line of sight or hovering on the periphery. She looked like a bright golden bird, the folds of her pale blue muslin gown fluttering in the light breeze, and try as he might, his wayward gaze kept wandering back to the corner where she stood with her sisters.

Lady Tremblay might scoff all she liked at their gowns, but he'd never seen the sisters look as well as they did this morning. In the years since his father had dragged him away from Kent they'd blossomed as surely as the wildflowers they'd once gathered in the meadow.

Their gowns were simple, yes, but they didn't need the extravagant adornments so many ladies of the *ton* relied upon. His gaze landed once again on Hattie, her cheeks pink from laughing at some nonsense of Egerton's. Her only ornamentation was a lace fichu, and a dark blue ribbon woven amongst her fair curls.

He'd missed her. There was no denying it. Seeing her now with her bluebell-blue eyes alight with laughter was like seeing a dream he'd had a thousand times come to life before his eyes.

She'd at last ceased writing to him after he'd stopped replying. It had been months since he'd had a letter from her, but it felt much longer than that, the emptiness that had once been filled by her letters an endless ache inside him.

But it was better this way, better if they didn't write to each other any longer, and better if they weren't friends, because sooner or later she'd end up regretting her association with him. One way or another, their friendship would end up hurting her.

Or so he'd told himself, but now...

It was one thing to give her up when he hadn't seen her in years, but she was here now, and it was like looking through a window into the past, into a brief time when she'd been his best friend, and he'd been happy.

But that was before he'd been crowned his father's heir. It didn't matter that it was a crown he'd never asked for, and one he'd never wanted. It was his now, and his father had spent the past twelve years of his life making certain he understood what was expected of the Earl of Windham.

The title was all that mattered now. That, and the money.

"Good morning, Windham. How do you do?"

Cass tore his gaze away from Hattie, and turned to find Magnus Sedgewick, Lord Pembroke standing beside him, one of Lady Farthingale's absurdly tiny glasses clutched awkwardly in his big paw.

"Pembroke. It's good to see you. I didn't know you were in London."

"I just arrived two days ago." Pembroke glanced around at Lady Farthingale's guests, his expression glum. "I've come for the season, and I don't mind telling you, Windham, I'm rather regretting it."

"Garden parties not your sort of thing, Pembroke?" Pembroke was a decent fellow, but he was rather stern, and a trifle stodgy for such a young man, and thus not a favorite with the *ton*.

"Not at all, no. Not garden parties, London, or the season, I'm afraid." His eye caught something over Cass's shoulder then, and his eyebrows rose. "Although perhaps I've spoken too soon."

Or rather, someone. Margaret Parrish.

"You wouldn't happen to be acquainted with that young lady, would you, Windham? The one in the green dress, standing next to Lady Fosberry?"

"In fact, I am acquainted with her. That young lady is Margaret Parrish. She's the eldest of Lord Melrose's younger sisters. Shall I introduce you?"

"That would be kind of you."

"Of course." It was a stroke of good luck, as it gave him an opportunity to warn Egerton, who was still hanging about Hattie like an unpleasant smell, to cast his nets elsewhere.

"...fascinating, Lady Harriet," Egerton was saying as Cass and Pembroke approached the group. "Do tell me more about the lectures, won't you? I've always been fascinated with horticulture."

God above, what utter bollocks. Egerton couldn't tell a daisy from a rose. "Are you really, Egerton? How curious. I've known you for years, and I don't recall you ever mentioning a single word about horticulture."

"Windham." Egerton's lip curled. "Where did you come from?"

"The other side of the lawn, Egerton. I should think that would be obvious." Cass didn't quite turn his back on Egerton, but it was a near thing. "Lady Fosberry, are you acquainted with Lord Pembroke?"

"Only by name. Lord Pembroke, how do you do?" Lady Fosberry offered Pembroke one of her most gracious smiles. "May I present my young friends to you, my lord? These ladies are Lord Melrose's sisters. Lady Sarah, Lady Harriet, and Lady Margaret."

"My pleasure, ladies," Pembroke murmured politely, but he was looking at Margaret when he said it.

"Lord Pembroke." She nodded shyly at him, her cheeks coloring prettily.

"The ladies and gentlemen are forming pairs for the lilac walk." Hayward held out his arm to Sarah Parrish. "Would you do me the honor of accompanying me, Lady Sarah? With Lady Fosberry's permission, of course."

"Yes, yes." Lady Fosberry waved them away. "Do go on, Sarah."

Sarah cast a quick glance at her eldest sister, but she couldn't refuse without being dreadfully rude, and she turned to Hayward with a smile. "Yes, of course, my lord."

Margaret's flushed cheeks paled as she watched them go, but she recovered quickly when Lord Pembroke offered her his arm with a smile. "May I escort you, Lady Margaret?"

"It would be my pleasure, my lord."

Cass hadn't spoken a word to Hattie. He hadn't even dared to look at her, certain his expression would give him away, yet somehow he knew what was about to unfold, as if it had already happened.

Then, in the next moment, it did.

Egerton gave Hattie his oiliest smile, opened his mouth, and said, "Lady Harriet would you do me the honor of—"

That was as far as he got.

"I'm afraid that's out of the question, Egerton." Before he knew what he was about to do, Cass stepped smoothly between Hattie and Egerton before Egerton could lay claim to her arm. "Lady Harriet has already agreed to accompany me on the lilac walk."

Without another word, he took Hattie's arm and led her away.

SEVEN

"I never agreed to accompany you on the lilac walk, Lord Windham. Indeed, I don't believe I've even bid you a good morning."

How could she have done? He'd seen her when she arrived—she was certain of it—but he'd kept as far away from her as possible. He hadn't spared her a single word or glance all morning, but she'd known where he was at every moment.

The lawn, the terrace, or fetching lemonade. It didn't matter where he was, or what he was doing. She was as aware of him as she was the warmth of the sun on her face.

It hurt, no longer being his friend. Perhaps she might have learned to live with it in time, though the space he'd once occupied in her heart would never have healed entirely. It would have always remained tender and bruised and achingly empty, but in time she would have reconciled herself to the loss of him.

But now, since she'd come to London they seemed to have somehow become enemies.

Was this how it would end? After twelve years of friendship and dozens upon dozens of letters, was it truly going to end like this?

It might have been easier if she'd understood why it had happened, but he'd simply vanished on her, more than a decade of friendship over in the blink of an eye, and in its place, nothing but baffling silence. He hadn't bothered to answer any of her letters for months, but all at once he was adamant that he, and only he could escort her through the lilac walk.

His behavior made no sense, and she'd had quite enough of it. She'd simply repeat herself until he answered her. "I never agreed to accompany you—"

"Yes, I'm aware of that, Lady Harriet, and I beg your pardon, but I won't leave you at the mercy of Lord Egerton."

"I'd hardly be at his mercy, my lord. It's a stroll among the lilacs, not a duel to the death. As for Lord Egerton, he appears to be a perfectly respectable gentleman."

"He isn't." Cass's voice was flat. "He's neither respectable, nor a gentleman."

If he was as wicked as Cass made him out to be, then why was he here at Lady Farthingale's garden party at all? "Lady Fosberry doesn't seem to share your opinion. If Lord Egerton is as awful as you say, she would have warned me away from him."

"I doubt she knows the truth about him. Lord Egerton is a master at dissembling. Trust me when I say you need to keep well away from him."

She had trusted him, once. There'd been a time when she'd trusted him more than anyone else in the world, a time when he'd been her best friend, but that time had passed.

"I know you don't trust me anymore," he added, with that uncanny knack he'd always had of knowing what she was thinking even before she knew it herself. "But I wouldn't lie to you, Hattie."

Hattie. Not Lady Harriet, but Hattie.

A crack in his armor, at last! Oh, it was a tiny one, to be sure, but even the tiniest crack eventually gave way to pressure. This was what she'd come to London for, this moment right here. This was a chance for her to talk to him, and she might not get a second one.

But where to begin? What were the right words to say to remind him who he'd once been? "The lilacs are lovely, are they not?" It wasn't an auspicious start, but their friendship had begun with a daisy crown.

Why should it not resume with lilacs?

"Lady Fosberry said all the *ton* pants for an invitation to Lady Farthingale's garden party," she went on. "Now I've seen her lilacs, I don't wonder at it."

Cass glanced around them, as if only just now noticing the lilacs. "I've always been fond of them, perhaps because they're one of the first flowers to bloom in the spring. They, ah...they put me in mind of the time I spent in Kent."

Kent. He was speaking to her of Kent. It was the very last thing she'd expected, and she was obliged to swallow before replying. Even so, when she spoke her voice wasn't quite steady. "But you've never seen the lilacs in Kent, Cass...I mean, Lord Windham. They were finished before you arrived that summer."

"The bluebells were finished as well. I distinctly remember Sarah lamenting that fact on that first day I spied on you. Neither cornflowers nor bellflowers would do for Lady Sarah, if I recall."

"No, and she remains quite as imperious as she was then." She hesitated, but the words were on the edge of her lips, and there was no holding them back. "Perhaps you should visit Kent in the spring sometime."

"Perhaps I should, but even though I never did get to see the bluebells in bloom in Kent, I can picture the great swaths of deep blue color set against a sea of green grass rippling in the wind. Whenever I see bluebells now, I think of that meadow."

The longing in his voice, the melancholy there...did he know he gave himself away with every syllable, every sigh, every word? But she wouldn't say so. The moment was too delicate, a mere wisp of a thing, and the wrong word might send it scattering like dandelion fluff.

"The meadow hasn't changed much since then. It's an ocean of wildflowers still."

"Or as Sarah would call them, weeds."

She laughed, giddy, her head spinning with bluebells and memories of Cass as he'd been then, a sweet, lost boy who was searching for a place to belong. "Well, to be fair, they *are* weeds."

"So, they are." He reached up to pluck one of the tiny blooms. It was more of a tunnel than a walk, with walls of lilacs on either side of them and hanging in dainty clusters above them. It was cool and quiet inside, as if they'd stumbled into their own private world.

"I shouldn't have..." He paused and blew out a breath. "I shouldn't have scolded you as I did in Lady Fosberry's garden yesterday. I was shocked to see you in Berkeley Square, and I didn't acquit myself as a gentleman ought to do. I beg your pardon."

His words were a balm to her bruised heart, and she let her eyes drop closed for an instant as they weaved a spell around her. But there were so many unanswered questions between them still, and nothing would ever be right again until she asked the one that made it feel as if the weight of the world had settled on her chest.

The one that had broken her heart.

"Why did you stop writing to me, Cass?"

He didn't answer her, not at once, but brought the blooms to his nose and inhaled, drinking them in as the silence lingered between them, as heavy as the sweet scent of lilacs.

Finally, he tossed the bloom aside and turned to face her, and his eyes...dear God, but there was a world of pain in those dark depths that astonished her.

"I'm the Earl of Windham, Hattie, and the Windham earls are not good men. A friendship with me would only end up hurting you. You deserve better than that."

There it was, the answer to the question she'd asked herself a thousand times, the question she'd shed a thousand bitter tears over. Perhaps it should have comforted her to have the answer at last, but it didn't.

It broke her heart all over again.

"You don't get to decide that for me, Cass." She grabbed his arm, her fingers tightening until somehow the fine material of his coat was twisted in her clenched fist. "You don't get to throw away twelve years of friendship as if it meant nothing to you."

"Is that what you think, Hattie? You think it meant nothing to me? It meant *everything*, but it's better this way, better if we don't—"

"No, it isn't! How can it be better for us to no longer be friends?"

"It's not as simple as—"

"You're not like your father, Cass! You may be the Earl of Windham now, but you *are* a good man." She clutched his coat, her eyes holding his, because maybe if she could make him look at her, he'd see the truth in her face.

"You don't understand, Hattie—"

"I do! I understand everything. I *know* you, Cass. I know you better than anyone else ever has or ever will." She slid her hand to the center of his chest and rested it there, over his heart. "I know you *here*, inside your heart."

She had the bluest eyes he'd ever seen. Years ago, he'd looked into her eyes, and something had clicked into place inside him. He'd been hardly more than a child then, but even so, he'd known he'd never again find eyes as blue as Hattie Parrish's.

Not cornflower, or bellflower, or even bluebell-blue, but a

blue all her own, such a deep blue looking into them was like hurling himself into the ocean.

Her eyes had ruined him for every other pair of blue eyes in England.

He shouldn't touch her. Touching her would only confuse things, and it was already so complicated between them, but he was reaching for her, and then he was touching her, her smooth cheek warm against the palm of his hand.

He gazed down into the endless blue of her eyes. "Tell me what you're really doing in London, Hattie. I know you too well to believe you came for the season."

"W-why..." She cleared her throat, the slender line of her neck moving in a rough swallow. "Why else would I have come?"

"You tell me." He caught a lock of her hair between his fingers, unable to resist caressing the silky strands. "The truth this time, Hattie."

"I—I already told you the truth."

She hadn't. He knew her words for a lie before they were even out of her mouth. She'd never been able to lie to him. "Tell me again."

She closed her eyes, her eyelashes brushing her flushed cheeks, but when she opened them again she met his gaze, and for an instant he was in Kent again with the thick branches of her brother's beech tree swaying between them.

"I-I came for the season, and...and to hear Sir Joseph Banks."

If he hadn't known her as well as he did he might have believed her, but even after a decade apart, he knew her as well as if he'd spent his entire lifetime with her.

She did know his heart, just as she said she did, but he knew hers, as well. "You've never been much of a liar, Hattie."

He'd meant to chastise her, to talk some sense into both of them, but his low, hoarse voice sounded like a caress, and she was so close, and somehow, despite every promise he'd made to himself, against reason and logic and every one of his better angels, he gave in to the moment, cradled her face in his hands and lowered his mouth to hers.

She made a soft sound, a sigh, a warm puff of breath against his lips, but she didn't draw away from him. He told himself to release her, but it was already too late for that.

It was madness, the risk they were taking, but now he had her in his arms, he couldn't let her go.

It was a shy kiss, a hesitant one, the kiss of an innocent, but the moment her soft lips touched his he was desperate for her, lost to her, every inch of him shuddering into aching awareness.

He eased her closer and opened his mouth over hers. A soft whimper left her throat, but she didn't pull away from him. Instead, her lips met his in a shy caress that set his blood on fire.

There wasn't a hint of resistance in her kiss. Her mouth went soft and pliant against his, and God, she was sweet, the sweetest thing he'd ever tasted. Had he known she would be? Hadn't he known, somehow, that as soon as he tasted her, he'd never be able to get enough of her?

He brushed his tongue against the seam of her lips, coaxing her to open for him, to give him everything.

Her hands flew to his chest, her fingers curling into his

waistcoat, and he couldn't keep himself from sliding his hands into the silky hair at the back of her neck. He drew her tighter against him, a low groan rumbling in his chest as he darted his tongue over the delicious curve of her lower lip.

Anyone might have stumbled upon them—even now the echo of footsteps and the faint strains of laughter reached them in their tiny, wooded alcove—but God help him, he couldn't make himself release her. Not yet, not when she was sighing for him, and the scent of lilacs was swimming in his head.

Nothing in the world could have made him release her.

As if in a dream he watched his hands slide around her waist, urging her closer, closer, until the tempting curve of her thighs was pressed against his pantaloons.

Did she feel it, too? This desire pulsing between them? Twelve years had passed, but the connection between them was as strong as it had ever been. Stronger, even, because there was no childlike innocence there, now. What had once been a sweet friendship had given way to something more, something deeper.

She hesitated for an instant, her soft, panting breaths fanning against his damp lips, and he forced himself to be still, to let her decide, but he couldn't restrain his growl of satisfaction when she traced his lower lip with a delicate stroke of her tongue, then pressed closer to meet him in a kiss that left him panting for breath.

"Hattie..." His voice was so guttural he hardly recognized it as his own. She was bewitching him with every brush of her mouth against his. Her arms slid around his neck, her fingers sinking into his hair and her body pressing closer until her breasts were crushed against his chest, and he...God help him, but he was ready to devour her.

Over a kiss. Just a kiss. He was no green lad who'd never known a woman's kiss.

He'd kissed dozens of ladies, but it had never been like this.

How could it be? None of them had been *her*.

Her scent, sunshine and grass and a faint hint of honeysuckle, the sweet curves of her body, her plump lips and tempting tongue...

She was driving him mad.

He trailed his fingertip down her cheek, pausing to caress her pouting lower lip and traced the smooth, pale skin of her neck before dropping a soft kiss in the shallow hollow at the base of her throat, tasting the wild flutter of her pulse against his tongue.

"You're beautiful, Hattie. You've always been beautiful."

"No, I—"

"Yes, you are." He pressed a finger to her lips, hushing her. "You are, Hattie."

He had no business touching her like this. He'd taken far too many liberties already, but releasing her now, while she was looking up at him with those half-lidded, sleepy blue eyes was impossible.

"Come here." Gently he turned them so her back was resting against the silvery trunk of a lilac tree. A shower of lilac petals fell around her, and she looked like a flower herself standing amongst the pale purple blooms, the filtered sunlight catching the strands of gold in her hair.

He traced the edge of the dainty lace fichu she'd tucked

into her bodice, his fingers moving slowly back and forth, his eyes dropping closed for an instant at the hint of warmth from her skin. He searched her face for any hint of reluctance, but there was nothing but heat in those lovely blue depths. "May I, Hattie?"

Her lips parted, her chest moving in quick panting breaths. "Yes."

No hesitation, and no doubt.

He eased the bit of lace aside, his breath quickening when the bare skin of her neck and throat was revealed. "So lovely. So pale and fine."

He traced the delicate line of her neck with one reverent finger, closing his eyes at the sensation of her smooth skin sliding against his fingertips.

And dear God, he was greedy, because he wanted more of her.

All of her.

But he paused when he reached the edge of her bodice, his gaze meeting hers. She was an innocent young lady, and he wouldn't frighten her for the world. "May I touch you here?"

Her eyes darkened to two twin pools of deep sapphire. She didn't answer with words, but took his hand and, holding his gaze, brought it to the edge of her bodice. Her skin was flushed, and underneath the filmy, pale blue linen of her bodice her nipples had gone tight.

She was a vision with the flush blooming on her pale skin and those blue eyes, her full lower lip caught in her teeth, and he'd never been good at practicing restraint.

But he would. For her, he would. He'd do anything for her.

He let his fingers wander over the pretty band of darker blue ribbon around her neckline and down the impossibly soft skin of her throat, and then, slowly...slowly, he reached for her, cupping her breasts in his palms.

Perfect. The breathless sigh that fell from her lips when he touched her, the flood of pink across the pale skin of her chest, the soft roundness of her cradled in his hands...perfection. Her nipples were hard for him, the stiff peaks pressing into his palms, and he couldn't tear his gaze away from her.

He'd never seen anything as lovely as her. She was a gift made for him alone.

But nothing had changed. She was everything that was good and true, and he...well, he was the Earl of Windham.

Arrogant, wicked, debauched. A villain, just as his father had been.

But like his father he was selfish, and he couldn't let her go any more than he could make his lungs cease to draw breath or force his heart to stop beating.

He brushed his thumb over her lower lip, smothering a groan when she parted for him, and a hint of dampness lingered there.

If a man could die of desire, then Hattie Parrish was going to be the end of him.

But this was a garden party, and there were dozens of people wandering about just on the other side of the lilac tree, any one of whom might turn the corner at any moment and see—

They were in Lady Farthingale's garden.

Dear God, had he lost his mind? If anyone had seen them duck into this alcove, or had noticed their prolonged absence, Hattie's reputation would be irreparably ruined.

And that...no. That couldn't happen.

"Hattie. Look at me." He caught her chin between his fingers and raised her face to his. "We shouldn't...we'll be missed soon. I need to take you back to Lady Fosberry."

She gazed up at him, the haze of desire slowly fading from her eyes. "Yes, I...yes, of course we...we should return at once."

But they didn't return to Lady Fosberry. Not right away. They remained as they were, with his arms around her and her hands resting on his chest, alone in a lilac-scented cocoon, the birds fluttering their wings as they sipped nectar from the blossoms.

EIGHT

Could anyone tell by looking at her that she'd just been thoroughly kissed?

Did her face, her burning cheeks give her away? No, no, such a thing must be impossible. No gentleman's kiss was so powerful that traces of it lingered on a lady's face after the kiss had ended.

But as she and Cass made their way from the lilac walk back to Lady Farthingale's terrace with the weight of dozens of gazes upon them it felt as if the kisses she and Cass had just shared were no longer a secret between the two of them.

Her lips felt swollen, sensitive, and with every step they took across the lawn her cheeks burned hotter, until it felt as if flames had engulfed her face.

"You've gone scarlet," Cass murmured to her as they approach the terrace. "I've never seen a prettier blush in my life, but there's no need for it. You've done nothing to be ashamed of, Lady Harriet."

Ashamed? No, perhaps not that. She could never be

ashamed of kissing Cass, but they were the last couple to emerge from the lilac walk, and if she could judge by the dismay on Margaret's face, not by an insignificant amount of time.

Oh, dear God. What had she done—

"Here you are, my dear." Lady Fosberry held out her hand to Hattie as she and Cass mounted the stairs and joined their party on the terrace. Her ladyship's smile was as calm as ever, but her knowing gaze lingered on Hattie's face, and Lord Hayward seemed to be scrutinizing her with more attention than usual, a slight frown furrowing his brow as he glanced between her and Cass.

"I was just telling your sisters that Lady Dumfries has graciously invited us to attend her ball next week. It's one of the most anticipated events of the season, and quite grand, indeed. I think we should—"

"Windham! Yoo-hoo, Lord Windham!" A lady was bearing down on them, and she wore a rather frightening look on her face, as if she were attempting to smile, but her lips were refusing every expression but a grimace. "My goodness, my lord, we've been searching for you everywhere. Where did you wander off to for such an age?"

"I beg your pardon, Lady Tremblay." Cass offered the ladies a polite bow, but no explanation of his whereabouts, and an awkward silence settled over the group.

Lady Tremblay wasn't a large personage, but she was so puffed up with prickly self-importance she put Hattie in mind of a porcupine on the verge of releasing its quills.

"No matter, Windham." A dark-haired young lady

followed on Lady Tremblay's heels. "Lord Egerton was kind enough to escort me through the lilac walk."

She strolled up the steps onto the terrace on Lord Egerton's arm as if she were a queen ascending her throne. She was the same lady Cass had been waiting on yesterday in Berkeley Square.

Lady Laetitia, presumably.

Her chilly blue gaze swept over the party before landing on Hattie. "Will you not introduce us to your friends, Windham?"

Cass looked as if he'd rather swallow his own tongue than make the introductions, but he offered Lady Laetitia the same courtly bow he'd given her mother. "Lady Tremblay and Lady Laetitia, may I present Lady Margaret, Lady Harriet and Lady Sarah Parrish."

"Lord Melrose's sisters, I believe? How lovely." Lady Tremblay gave them a brief but poisonous smile that belied her words before turning her attention to Lady Fosberry. "Did I not just hear you say, Patience, that you plan to attend Lady Dumfries's ball next week?"

Lady Fosberry had never been one to be intimidated by the *ton*, and she wasn't intimidated now. "No, indeed. I'm afraid you misheard, Josephine, but then that's what comes of eavesdropping." She offered Lady Tremblay a poisonous smile of her own. "I was merely telling my young friends Lady Dumfries invited us, nothing more."

"How tremendously kind of Lady Dumfries. But haven't you only just returned to Town? I daresay your friends haven't yet acquired the proper clothing." Lady Tremblay made a great show of looking Hattie up and down. "Such a pity, as it means you can't attend."

A flush rose in Cass's cheeks. "That's absurd. I don't see why—"

"It's quite all right, Lord Windham. Dear Lady Tremblay is only looking out for us, isn't that right, Josephine?" Lady Fosberry turned her iciest smile on Lady Tremblay, her teeth gleaming. "I do so appreciate your concern, my lady, but you needn't worry yourself. My friends have everything they need."

"Why, my dearest Patience, of course, they do, but as you said yourself, Lady Dumfries's ball is quite grand, and it's only a week away. Alas, there's no time to have any gowns made up."

"Gowns?" Lord Hayward stared at her, baffled. "I daresay these young ladies have brought plenty of gowns from Kent that will do for the ball."

"Kent!" Lady Tremblay laughed. "My dear Lord Hayward, don't be absurd! These young ladies are Lord Melrose's sisters! I'm certain they'd never dream of appearing at a *ton* ball in their provincial fashions, as it won't reflect well on their brother. Patience, I know you're much too kind to wish to see your little friends humiliated."

Lady Tremblay was obliged to make a great effort to hide her delight at that prospect. As for Lady Laetitia, she said nothing, but the slight sneer on her lips gave her away more quickly than any words could.

"Nonsense," Lord Hayward said shortly. "You must come. In fact, will you do me the honor of dancing the first dance with me, Lady Sarah?"

"How kind you are, my lord." Sarah bit her lip, her glance straying toward Margaret.

"Of course, you must, Sarah."

Margaret gave Sarah a bright smile that likely fooled everyone else, but not Hattie. Margaret looked so downcast, in fact, a prickle of unease darted up her spine.

Was Lord Hayward the reason Margaret had agreed to come to London with so little fuss? Was Margaret nursing a *tendre* for the handsome young earl? She'd known Lord Hayward was in Town from Alice Weatherby's letters to Sarah.

She glanced at Margaret, her heart sinking as she read the truth on her sister's face.

Lord Hayward, it seemed, had made quite an impression on fifteen-year-old Margaret.

Now here he was, mooning over Sarah like a besotted schoolboy. Dash it, why could things never work out as they were meant to?

The worst of it was, Sarah couldn't refuse Lord Hayward's invitation to dance—not without forfeiting the chance to dance entirely, and Margaret would never doom her beloved youngest sister to being a wallflower at her very first ball.

"Very well, then. It would be my pleasure, Lord Hayward."

Sarah gave his lordship a pretty curtsey, but she looked nearly as downcast as Margaret. Fortunately, Lord Pembroke, who hadn't ventured a word since they'd all returned from the lilac walk spoke up then. "May I have your first dance, Lady Margaret?"

Oh, bless the man! If Hattie could have hugged him, she would have.

Margaret clearly hadn't expected this, and her cheeks went as red as a peony, but she murmured a shy assent, and it all might have ended happily enough if Lord Egerton hadn't opened his mouth.

"All three of Lord Melrose's sisters must dance!" He turned to Hattie with a gallant bow. "Indeed, Lady Harriet, you can hardly refuse me your first two dances."

Beside her, Cass made a strange noise, a low, rumbling sound that came from the pit of his chest. It was rather like a...

My goodness, had Cass just *growled*? Because it had sounded very much like a growl.

"I, ah..." Oh, no. What was she to do? She glanced at Lady Fosberry, but there was little her ladyship could do, and she gave a helpless shrug.

Goodness, what a conundrum!

Cass had gone out his way to warn her against Lord Egerton, so she could only assume he wouldn't be pleased if she accepted the man's invitation, but Lord Egerton had behaved with perfect respect toward her.

With kindness, even. She had no reason in the world to refuse him.

"Yes, of course, I'd be pleased to dance with you, my lord."

Cass said nothing, but beside her he was fuming with such intensity she could almost see steam pouring out of his ears. Meanwhile, Lord Egerton was ecstatic, and not a little smug. "I look forward to it, Lady Harriet."

"It seems the question of whether we will attend has been resoundingly answered, has it not, Lady Tremblay?" Lady Fosberry didn't bother to hide the triumph in her voice. "But not to worry, Josephine. I'll endeavor to see that my young friends are properly attired."

Lady Tremblay's face had flushed an unattractive shade of red. "How wonderful for your little friends, Patience. We look forward to seeing you there." She seized her daughter's arm.

"Come along, Laetitia."

"It's wonderful to have you back in Town, Lady Fosberry." Lord Hayward was positively gleeful as he watched Lady Tremblay march off in a huff. "There's no better entertainment in London than watching you put Josephine Tremblay in her place."

"Nonsense, Lord Hayward. I have no idea what you mean." Lady Fosberry drew herself up, but a smile lingered at the corners of her lips. "Come, girls, bid their lordships goodbye, and we'll be on our way. We've rather a lot of shopping to do, you know!"

Before Hattie could follow, Cass caught her elbow and drew her a little apart from the group. "You aren't dancing with Lord Egerton, Lady Harriet."

If he'd been a touch less demanding, her hackles might not have risen as they did, but Cass had grown a great deal more arrogant since he'd become a lord. Or perhaps it wasn't that, at all. Perhaps he'd simply grown accustomed to speaking in just the same way his father had spoken to him.

But it wouldn't do. Everyone else might bow and scrape before the mighty Lord Windham, but she would not have him ordering her about. It was bad enough he'd tried to order her to leave London, but now he thought he could dictate which gentleman she could and could not dance with?

"On the contrary, my lord, I certainly will dance with him. I've already said I would, and I won't go back on my promise. I realize you're not fond of Lord Egerton, but—"

"I'm not fond of him because he's a villain, Hattie. I won't have you—"

"It's nothing to do with you." She snatched her elbow out of his grip. "In any case, it's a dance, Lord Windham, not a betrothal."

Cass dragged a hand through his hair, setting the dark strands on end, and for an instant, with his hair freed from its ruthlessly fashionable style, she saw a hint of the boy she'd once loved so well.

He was still there, hiding underneath Lord Windham's cool, smooth surface, and even that brief glimpse of him made her heart flutter in her chest. "It's not as if I'll be in any danger in a crowded ballroom, Cass."

"I don't like it, Hattie. I don't like it at all."

She shrugged. "You might have prevented it, you know."

He gave her a sulky look. "I don't see how."

"It's quite simple, Lord Windham. You might have asked me to dance yourself."

She didn't wait for his reply but turned on her heel and marched after Lady Fosberry and her sisters, but she couldn't quite smother a rush of satisfaction at his speechlessness.

Yes, a little humility would do very well for the handsome, elegant Earl of Windham.

As soon as they were all safely tucked into the privacy of Lady Fosberry's carriage, Sarah, who'd never been one to mince words asked, "Who was that awful woman and her equally awful daughter?"

"That's unkind of you, Sarah." But Margaret's scold was half-hearted, and she added, "They were rather dreadful, weren't they?"

"My dears, you have no idea. I assure you that Lady Tremblay is a plague upon London, and I'm not the only one who thinks so. She's the scourge of the *ton*, and her daughter, Lady Laetitia is scarcely any better, though she's more adept at hiding her vitriol than her mother is."

"Not that adept." Sarah fell back against the squabs with a huff. "She looked at Hattie as if she'd happily snatch every hair from her head. She's very pretty, but I'd wager my best bonnet she has an ugly heart."

"Yes, it's rather a dark, withered thing, I'm afraid." Lady Fosberry darted a glance at Hattie. "If the gossips are to be believed, Lord Windham is considering courting her this season."

Hattie froze. Had she heard that right? Cass, *courting* Lady Laetitia?

But that was impossible! Why, not half an hour ago he'd been kissing her most ardently in the lilac walk! What sort of gentleman kissed one lady while intending to soon begin courting another?

And why Lady Laetitia, of all people? Why, Cass had a nerve warning her away from Lord Egerton when he was considering courting such a viper as Lady Laetitia!

Was her face as red as the heat in her cheeks hinted it was?

It must have been, because Lady Fosberry hastened to add, "It's just gossip, and as likely to be nonsense as *ton* gossip generally proves to be. I believe Lord Windham's father favored the match."

"Yes, but he's dead, isn't he? I shouldn't think he'd have much say in it, being as dead as he is."

"Sarah!" Margaret turned to her sister, but a laugh escaped her before she could gather her breath to scold. "You're incorrigible."

"Well, my dears, we'll cross our fingers that it's just gossip." Lady Fosberry squeezed Hattie's hand. "Perhaps Lord Windham has made some mistakes, but he in no way deserves to be cursed with such an arrogant, disagreeable wife."

"No, indeed," Margaret replied, and Sarah nodded in agreement.

But Hattie didn't say a word.

It was true, what Lady Fosberry said. Cass deserved much better than Lady Laetitia, but even in death, his father still had a hold on him. The question was, how far beyond the grave would the late Earl of Windham's wickedness reach?

Cass's future happiness might depend on the answer.

She turned to gaze out the window, her head spinning as London rolled by on the other side of the glass.

"What the devil is going on between you and Lady Harriet, Windham?"

Of all the questions Hayward might have asked, he'd landed on the one Cass had no idea how to answer. So, he lied. "Not a thing. I have no idea what you're talking about, Hayward."

"No? That's odd, Windham. Indeed, the circumstances say otherwise."

"What circumstances?"

Hayward held up his hand and began counting points off on his fingers. "Let's see, shall we? First, you and Lady Harriet were the last to emerge from the lilac walk. Second, when you did emerge at last, she had the pink-cheeked charm of a lady who'd just been kissed. But I suppose you don't know anything about that, do you?"

Not only had Hattie looked as if she'd just been kissed, but quite thoroughly, at that. A bolt of pure lust shot through him at the memory of her reddened, kiss-swollen lips and hazy blue eyes, her slightly mussed golden hair.

What would that glorious hair look like tumbling down her back? Or spread across a pillow. She was so lovely, so tempting—

"Well, Windham? What have you got to say for yourself?"

There was no use denying it. Hayward could always tell when he was lying. "Do you think Lady Fosberry noticed it?"

"Of course, she did. Nothing gets past Lady Fosberry. Fortunately for you, I doubt anyone else did, and a damned good thing, too. For God's sake, Windham, do you care nothing for the lady's reputation?"

"I do, very much," he said quietly. "She...she matters a great deal to me, Hayward."

He cared more for Hattie than he'd ever cared for anyone, but he hadn't behaved as if he did, had he? He could trust Hayward to keep his secrets, but if Lady Fosberry had noticed, others might have, as well. Good God, he must have gone mad, kissing her as he had. What if someone had happened to see them?

Hayward's expression softened, but he wasn't yet prepared to let it go. "You have a perverse way of showing it, Windham. Lady Laetitia wasn't at all pleased, and neither was her mother."

"No. I'm certain they expected me to escort Laetitia through the lilac walk."

"Indeed, and neither of them are the sort to take disappointment lightly, something you may want to consider before you make up your mind to court her, Windham."

"I've considered it." He'd done little else but consider it. "My father—"

"Your father is dead, Windham." Hayward said flatly. "You owe him nothing. Certainly not a lifetime of misery."

Cass glanced at his friend in surprise. Hayward had never been an admirer of his father's, but neither had he stated his opinion so bluntly before.

Hayward sighed. "I beg your pardon, Windham. I only mean to say you needn't marry for money. But since we're speaking so frankly, what was that strange business with Egerton earlier? You nearly tore his head off when he tried to take Lady Harriet's arm."

"It's quite simple, Hayward. Egerton's a villain, and I don't want him anywhere near Lady Harriet or her sisters."

"Weren't you friends with him at one time?"

"Yes. I knew him at Eton, and later at Oxford."

"Go on then, Windham. What's Egerton done?"

Plenty, and every year more shocking than the last. Egerton, like so many men of the *ton* was not the proper gentleman he pretended to be.

But then Cass was no proper gentleman, either. If he'd had any real honor, Egerton's drinking, gaming and casual cruelty would have been enough to end their friendship.

It hadn't been. But then Egerton had done something Cass could never forgive. "He threatened Lady Harriet."

Hayward stared at him. "*Threatened* her?"

"Not directly. He didn't know it was her he was threatening. It's a trifle complicated."

"I have time." Hayward lounged back against the squabs and waved his hand. "Proceed."

"Lady Harriet and I kept in touch after I left Kent. We carried on a correspondence."

Hayward blinked. "You carried on a correspondence with a lady to whom you're not betrothed?"

"Yes. It went on for twelve years."

"Twelve...good God, Windham. Are you mad?"

Perhaps he was, a bit. At least, he was when it came to Hattie. "I had dozens of letters from her. No, hundreds. I kept them locked in my desk, but one night after drinking until the wee hours of the morning at White's, Egerton joined me at my townhouse for a glass of brandy. I fell asleep."

"Go on."

"When I woke I found Egerton sitting in my chair, his feet on my desk, happily reading through the letters Lady Harriet had sent me."

Hayward shot upright. "You mean to say he went through your private papers?"

"Yes. The letters were locked in my desk, but I'd carelessly left the key out, and he helped himself to it. He was vastly entertained by the letters. He even congratulated me on, as he put it, having 'a bird in the hand.'"

"That bloody villain! Was he...wait. Were the letters signed? Does Egerton know Lady Harriet is the one who—"

"No. She signed them with a childhood nickname. Egerton doesn't know Lady Harriet is the lady who wrote to me, but if he should ever find out—"

"He'll use it against her, as sure as we're both sitting here. The man has no conscience."

"None whatsoever. To make matters worse, Egerton's gaming has caught up to him. He's on the verge of ruin. He's come to London for the season because he must marry, and he must marry well."

"And here's Lady Harriet—sweet, beautiful, richly-dowered and innocent to the ways of London. Christ, Egerton must be salivating to get his hands on her. Do you think he would—"

"Use the letters to try and force her to marry him? I'm certain of it."

"But surely Lady Harriet wouldn't agree to—"

"She would if she believed it would affect her sisters' prospects if her own reputation was damaged." Hattie would never permit Margaret and Sarah to suffer for any action of hers. "Whatever else happens, Egerton can't ever find out Lady Harriet is the lady from my letters."

"We'll make certain of it, Windham. I promise it. Is there anything else?"

"No. That's the whole of it."

Or nearly the whole of it. He'd held one thing back. Something he couldn't bring himself to say aloud, not even to Hayward.

He hadn't wanted to stop writing to Hattie. It had nearly killed him to do it, but the day after Egerton had found those letters, he'd promised himself he'd cut all ties with her.

He wasn't good for Hattie. If the disaster with Egerton proved nothing else, it proved that. She hadn't been to London for years, yet her association with him had still put her reputation at risk.

It wouldn't happen a second time.

Hattie was the one pure, bright spot in a lifetime of excess and vice.

She was the only thing he'd ever done right.

He wouldn't see her hurt. Not by Egerton, and especially not by himself.

NINE

"My dear girls, welcome to the jewel of Mayfair." Lady Fosberry waved her hand with a flourish. "It's magnificent, is it not?"

"Magnificent, and enormous, my lady." Sarah clutched Lady Fosberry's arm. "Why, there must be hundreds of shops inside!"

"Don't be silly, child." Lady Fosberry gave Sarah's hand a fond pat. "There aren't hundreds. I believe there are only seventy-two at present."

"Seventy-two! Just think of all the silks and gloves and ribbons! And the hats—my goodness, my lady, the hats! I'd come here every single day if I lived in London, and I'd wear a different hat each time."

Hattie had heard of Burlington Arcade, of course. Everyone in England knew of it. But hearing about a thing and seeing it with one's own eyes were quite different experiences.

She'd never imagined it could be as grand as this.

They were standing at the north end of the building, on Burlington Gardens Street. Above them was an elegant trio of arches, each adorned with its own ornate gas lantern suspended from the center, and fashionable crowds of ladies and gentlemen roamed in and out of the pretty wrought iron gates underneath.

She'd never been fond of shopping—laces and ribbons and other fripperies bored her, but Burlington Arcade was a far cry from the tiny High Street in Chatham, and even she wasn't immune to the tantalizing glimpses of finery displayed behind endless sheets of polished glass.

"It's a lucky thing you don't live in London, Sarah, or our brother would end his days in the poorhouse." Margaret gave Sarah an indulgent smile. "Where shall we go first?"

"Let me think. We need new gowns for each of you, along with new stockings, slippers and gloves, and a jeweled headband for Sarah, and a wrap for Hattie. The one you've brought from Kent won't do for Lady Dumfries's ball, dear." Lady Fosberry tapped a gloved finger to her lips. "There's only one place that will do. Follow me, girls."

Lady Fosberry led them under the splendid arches and into the covered marble walkway. A slice of bright blue sky—rare for London in the spring—peeked through the glass roof above them, and for the first time since they'd left Lady Farthingale's garden party, Hattie's spirits lifted.

She had a dozen misgivings about their continued presence in London. Misgivings about lying to Johnathan, and about Lady Laetitia and her dreadful mother. Misgivings about Sarah and Lord Hayward, and Margaret and Lord Pembroke, and misgivings about Cass.

Dozens upon dozens of misgivings about Cass, and most particularly about his kiss.

She pressed her fingers to her lips, her cheeks heating at the memory of his mouth on hers. She'd kissed Cass. She'd *kissed* Cass, and the only thing that had been strange about it was that it hadn't felt strange, at all.

Although to be strictly truthful, Cass had kissed *her*, not the other way around, but it wasn't as if she'd pushed him away, was it? No, she'd most decidedly returned his kiss. Returned it with ardor, even, which was...well, a trifle embarrassing, really.

Not so embarrassing she wouldn't do it again, if the opportunity arose.

But if there was one place in London where a lady could put her worries behind her, it was at Burlington Arcade, especially with Sarah stopping to gasp at every glittering storefront.

"Madame Céline will take good care of us." Lady Fosberry swept along the path with her arm linked with Sarah's. "Madame Céline is all the rage in London this season, but she always makes time for me. There isn't another modiste with a more elegant taste than Madame Céline. Do come along, Sarah. We'll never get there if you insist on stopping at every shop."

Lady Fosberry took them deep into the arcade, past endless shops and around dozens of corners until the maze ended at last at an enormous glass window with *La Maison des Dames* in gold script scrolling across the front of it.

"Here we are, girls." She marched up to a long, polished glass counter where an elegant, dark-haired shopgirl was sorting silk ribbons. "Aimée, please tell Madame Céline I'm here with my charges to see them outfitted for Lady Dumfries's ball."

"Of course, my lady. Right away." Aimée smiled at them and hurried out from behind the counter. "Madame Céline is busy with Lady Tremblay and her daughter, but I'll tell her you're here. It won't be but a moment."

"Goodness, Lady Tremblay is the bad penny that keeps turning up, is she not, girls? Well, no matter. Shall we amuse ourselves with the ribbons until Madame Céline is available?"

Sarah and Margaret followed Lady Fosberry to the counter, but Hattie didn't have much interest in ribbons, so she wandered over to the plate glass window to look at a display of enormous ostrich plumes that had been dyed a most decadent purple, but she soon gave it up in favor of peeking at the fashionable people wandering by on the other side of the glass.

The ostrich plumes were the perfect cover from which to spy on them.

As it happened, there was a gentleman's tailor just opposite Madame Céline's shop. It was a formidable looking place, and frighteningly distinguished, with a smart store front done up in bottle green paint with "Gentleman's Sundries" written across the window in black lettering.

By the looks of it, every gentleman in London—young and old, plain and handsome, some in breeches and others in pantaloons, some wearing Hoby boots and others in Wellingtons—every sort of gentleman one could imagine seemed to have an urgent need of tailoring this afternoon.

There was even a gentleman who looked very much like...
Like the Earl of Windham.

She let out a little squeak, freezing in place for an instant like a frightened rabbit, but thankfully her wits returned in time for her to duck behind a pair of towering plumes, these ones dyed a shockingly bright pink.

It was ridiculous to hide from him, of course—she wasn't a child, for pity's sake—but what did a lady say to a gentleman who'd so thoroughly kissed her only days earlier? Particularly if said lady had been dreaming about that kiss since it happened?

It was much easier to hide, but alas, cowardice was always its own punishment, wasn't it?

The door to Madame Céline's opened just then and a group of chattering ladies entered, slamming the door behind them and setting the pink plumes aflutter. The movement caught Cass's attention as he passed, and it was all over for her, then.

He spied her at once, stopped, and then...

Then he did something she didn't expect.

He smiled at her. That wasn't so astonishing, although she'd had precious few of Cass's smiles since she'd arrived in London. It was the texture of it, the way it swept from his mouth to his eyes in an instant, as if it had taken over his face before he had a chance to think better of it.

This wasn't the arrogant Earl of Windham's smile. It was the grin she remembered from the brief summer they'd spent together. Wide, friendly, artless, and a touch mischievous...

It was *Cass's* smile.

She was helpless against that smile. Unbidden, an

answering grin curved her lips, and they stood there grinning at each other through the glass like a pair of fools until Cass regained his senses and entered the shop.

"Shopping for feathers Lady Harriet?" He raised an eyebrow at the pair of pink monstrosities. "Dear God, I've never seen such bright plumes in my life. They're rather terrifying."

"They are, indeed. Enormous, as well. What does one do with such large plumes, do you suppose?"

"Put them on ladies' hats, I believe, but I don't think..." He glanced from the plumes to her face, his lips twitching. "But I don't think these particular plumes will suit you, Lady Harriet."

"No, they're far too grand for me. I'm not partial to plumes, in any case."

"But a bonnet must have the proper trimmings, mustn't it? How about these, instead?" He plucked a slender egret feather dyed a deep blue from a display of feathers in a glass jar. "How about this one? It's much daintier than the other, and this blue is the exact shade of your eyes."

He hadn't meant to say it. That was evident by the way his eyes widened as soon as the words left his lips, and his cheeks...goodness, was he blushing? Cassian Fitzgerald, the Earl of Windham, *blushing*?

No, surely not. She must be imagining it.

She took the feather to have a closer look, then shook her head, and dropped it back into the jar. "It's very pretty, and just the sort of feather I'd choose if I wore feathers at all, but I'm content with plain ribbons, my lord. They're not as dramatic as ostrich plumes. I'm afraid I'm quite dull, but plain ribbons suit me."

"They do," he murmured, his dark gaze searching her face. "And you're not dull, Hattie. Indeed, it's just the opposite. There's not a single thing about you that isn't engaging."

Did Cass truly find her engaging? She opened her mouth to ask him, but thankfully he interrupted her before she could embarrass herself with such a ridiculous question.

"So, Lady Harriet, how does your brother do?"

"My brother?" What did Johnathan have to do with anything?

"Yes. Lord Melrose." Cass's eyes were twinkling. "You do remember him, do you not?"

"Of course, I—"

"I trust he and Lady Melrose had a pleasant trip from Kent?"

Oh, no. "Er, yes, very pleasant. He's...ah, that is, he and Lady Melrose are very well."

"Wonderful! Then I'll call on him tomorrow morning, shall I?"

"No, tomorrow won't do. He's...they...we're...that is, we're—"

"Hattie?"

"Yes?"

"Lord and Lady Melrose aren't coming to London, are they?"

Dash it. "No."

"No. I thought not." He stepped closer to her, his gaze

dropping to her lips. "I've told you before, Hattie. You're a dreadful liar."

He was thinking about the kiss. She knew it as surely as if he'd said so aloud. Warmth flooded her cheeks, and the next thing she knew she'd mirrored his actions by taking a step toward him, until they were so close she caught the faintest hint of bay from his cologne.

The scent, warmed by his skin, was...God above, but she wanted to roll around in it, bathe in it.

"Hattie, I need to tell you—"

"Lord Windham! Yoo-hoo, Lord Windham!"

They sprang apart. There, bearing down on them like a runaway carriage was Lady Tremblay, a footman loaded with paper wrapped parcels trailing in her wake. "Lord Windham, what luck! Laetitia, wherever have you disappeared to? Do come here, dearest, and bid Lord Windham a good after—"

She broke off as she caught sight of Hattie, her smile transforming into such a fierce frown Hattie took an instinctive step backward. "Lady Harriet. I didn't see you there."

"Lady Tremblay." Hattie dipped into a polite curtsey.

"My, you do have a habit of turning up when one least expects it, don't you?" Lady Tremblay didn't wait for a reply, but turned to Cass with a flounce, a bright, false smile on her face.

"We've just had Laetitia's final fitting, and I daresay you won't be able to take your eyes off her at Lady Dumfries's ball, my lord. But then she *is* the season's belle." Lady Tremblay glanced at Hattie, her eyes narrowed. "No other young lady compares to her."

"My goodness, such an exaggeration, mamma!" Lady Laetitia appeared suddenly, emerging from behind a display of gloves tucked into one corner of the shop. "I doubt Lord Windham will even notice me."

"Don't be absurd, Laetitia. There isn't a gentleman in London who hasn't noticed you." Lady Tremblay inserted herself between Cass and Hattie and lowered her voice. "I won't give away the surprise by telling you the color of her gown, but it's the height of fashion, I assure you, my lord."

"Then I'd be wise to solicit Laetitia's hand for the first two dances, before some other gentleman cuts me out." Cass offered Lady Laetitia a gallant bow, but all the animation that had been in his face moments before had fled, and his eyes had gone dull.

Neither Lady Laetitia nor her mother seemed to notice. Lady Tremblay shot Hattie a triumphant glance before turning back to Cass. "How gracious you are, my lord. Laetitia will be pleased to dance the first two dances with you, won't you, darling?"

"Of course, mamma." Laetitia lowered her eyes modestly, but there was a satisfied little smirk playing about her lips.

"Very good. Now that's settled, I'll take my leave. Lady Harriet."

Cass offered Hattie a curt bow, and then he was gone, the only indication he'd been there at all the scent of bay he left in his wake.

But there was no forgetting the way his smile had vanished when Lady Tremblay had called his name, and sadness overwhelmed her, leaving an aching, hollow pit in the center of her chest.

This was the lady that Cass was considering marrying. A lady who made the smile drop from his lips as if she'd torn it loose from his mouth with sharp, pointed claws. *This* was the family his father had chosen for him, dooming him to a lifetime of unhappiness.

Why would Cass have agreed to such a match? Perhaps he could fool everyone else, but she knew him too well to believe he was in love with Lady Laetitia Tremblay.

He didn't even *like* her, for pity's sake.

Why was he considering marrying her? To please his deceased father, a father who had never truly cared for him, who'd only ever seen Cass as a tool to secure the Windham name, fortunes and title?

Had his father brainwashed him to the point that Cass could no longer see how unhappy a marriage to Lady Laetitia would make him? Or was he punishing himself, because by some twisted logic he believed he no longer deserved happiness?

Oh, she didn't know! Even if she could make sense of it, what could she possibly do to help him—

"Lady Harriet! Are you listening to me? For pity's sake, girl you're a million miles away."

Hattie jerked back to attention to find Lady Tremblay frowning at her, her hands on her hips. "I beg your pardon, my lady. What were you saying?"

"Nothing of any consequence, only that I noticed a gown hanging in the back of Madame Céline's shop that would be just the thing for you." Lady Tremblay cast a calculating glance from her head to her toes, her eyes gleaming. "Yes, indeed, just the thing. Very flattering, indeed."

Hattie managed not to roll her eyes. Just the thing, indeed. If there'd been any way to manage it, Lady Tremblay would see to it she was forced to appear at Lady Dumfries's ball wearing a sackcloth and ashes.

But of course, she couldn't say so. Instead, she offered Lady Tremblay a polite nod. "Is there, indeed? How fortunate for me. I'll be sure to ask Madame Céline all about it."

"You do that, my dear. Come along, Laetitia." Lady Tremblay took Laetitia's arm and gestured imperiously at the footman waiting patiently behind her. "Come, James."

They sailed off without a backward glance, with James staggering along behind them.

She waited until they were gone, then hurried back to the window and peered out into the covered walkway in hopes she might find Cass there again, but there was no dark head towering above the rest of the crowd.

He was gone.

All at once, all the pleasure she'd been taking in the day vanished with him.

She wandered around the shop in search of Lady Fosberry, but she found only Aimée, who'd gone back to sorting her ribbons. She looked up when Hattie approached and offered her a smile. "Lady Harriet, there you are. Lady Fosberry has been asking for you. Follow me, please."

Lady Fosberry was enthroned on a white silk settee in a private little room at the back of the shop, watching as Sarah turned this way and that in front of an enormous looking glass. "Oh my, yes. Yes, that will do very well."

"Sarah?" Hattie gasped. "My goodness!"

Tears pricked her eyes as she gazed at her youngest sister whose health the entire family had once despaired of.

There was no trace of Sarah's childhood illness now. She was pink-cheeked and radiant and terribly grown up as she gazed into the glass, as if she couldn't quite believe it was her own reflection staring back at her. "Is it all right?"

"All right? My dear child, it's a good deal better than that." Lady Fosberry nodded with satisfaction. "That shade of pale pink is utter perfection on you, Sarah."

"Hattie?" Sarah turned toward her, the silk skirts rustling. "What do you think?"

Good God, but she was going to cry. She was going to burst into tears right here in *Le Maison des Dames*. She drew closer and took Sarah's face in her hands. "I think you look beautiful, Sarah."

"Thank you," Sarah whispered, and pressed a kiss to Hattie's cheek before turning back to the glass with a soft sigh.

"I believe we've found something for Margaret, as well. It's the most delicious shade of primrose imaginable. She looks like an angel in it."

Margaret was an angel, so that made perfect sense. "I'm sure she does. Lady Tremblay advised me to ask Madame Céline about a gown she's set aside back here. I daresay whatever it is, it will prove uniquely unflattering."

"No doubt Lady Tremblay thinks so. I've already seen the gown. Madame Céline made it for Lady Laetitia, but she rejected it on the grounds that it's not the right shade of blue. It errs on the side of Prussian blue, and Lady Laetitia wanted Celestial blue."

"Every young lady in London wants Celestial blue."

"Indeed, because it flatters everyone, whereas only ladies of a certain complexion can wear Prussian blue. Ladies like you, for instance."

"Prussian blue? Isn't that shade too bright to be proper for a young lady?"

Lady Fosberry waved this away. "My dear Hattie, you'd be amazed at how quickly propriety gives way to vanity."

"What does that mean?"

"Just this. When a gown flatters a lady, no one cares a whit about the rules. Perhaps it's not strictly appropriate for your first ball, but this is London, my dear. Beauty and fashion override all else."

"But why would Lady Tremblay suggest a gown that will flatter me? She's made no secret of her dislike."

"No, Josephine isn't at all subtle, is she? Come here, dear, and sit down." Lady Fosberry patted the place next to her on the settee. "Bright shades wash Laetitia out, you see. No doubt Lady Tremblay thinks it will do the same to you."

Hattie plopped down onto the settee. "You don't agree?"

"I do not. I have an inkling, Hattie, that you'll be utterly devastating in Prussian blue."

TEN

C ass had heard the Sussex Waltz played dozens of times, but never had it been as interminable as it was tonight. It went on forever, the violins grating against his eardrums, the endless plink of the piano keys echoing in his head.

No one else seemed to notice it.

Not Hayward, who was dancing with Lady Sarah and wearing a grin that hinted he'd happily listen to a dozen Sussex Waltzes playing end to end if it meant keeping the lady in his arms.

Not Lord Pembroke, who'd abandoned his usual stiff propriety as he squired a pink-cheeked Lady Margaret around the ballroom, his own face flushed with pleasure.

And certainly not Lord Egerton, who looked as satisfied as a snake who'd just swallowed a rat, now that he had Hattie in his arms.

There was only one person in Lady Dumfries's ballroom who was even less satisfied than he was, and that was Lady

Laetitia Tremblay. If the scowl on her face was any indication, she was only a few plinks of the piano away from giving
way to a temper tantrum.

"For pity's sake, Windham!" she hissed. "I don't know
why you solicited my hand for the first two dances if you
intended to ignore me the entire time."

Good God, but she was tiresome. How had he overlooked
it for so long?

"I beg your pardon, my lady."

His apology didn't appease Laetitia, of course. Mottled
red stained her cheeks, and she went on with her harangue
as if he hadn't spoken, her temper rising with every word.
"You haven't said a word about my gown. Four yards of
French lace, Windham. Four yards, and not one word!"

"You look ravishing, as always, Laetitia."

And she did. Laetitia was the season's belle for a reason.
She always looked ravishing, right up until the moment she
opened her mouth, and she hadn't closed it once since this
never-ending Sussex Waltz began.

Laetitia gave him a sulky look. "My gown is in the height
of fashion. It took Madame Céline ages to make it. Celestial
blue is all the rage this season, despite what *some* ladies
might think."

Ah, now they were getting to it.

There was little doubt which lady had earned Laetitia's
ire. He'd nearly swallowed his tongue when Hattie entered
the ballroom in her brilliant blue gown. He'd only caught the
briefest glimpse of her, but that was all it had taken.

She was every summer sky, every undulating ocean,

every meadow wildflower he'd ever seen, all at once. She was so lovely it made his chest ache to look at her.

And she was dancing with Egerton.

Not him, but Egerton, of all cursed people, and she'd be dancing with Egerton for all eternity by the looks of things, because this bloody waltz was never going to end. Around they went, skipping and twirling and spinning until Laetitia was thoroughly disgusted with him, and he was ready to scream.

Bloody Egerton. Just the sight of the man's face was enough to put him out of temper.

Lady Laetitia kept up her injured silence through the rest of the dance, but she wasn't one to hold her tongue for long. The dance did end at last, and the musicians launched at once into a rousing rendition of *La Pantalon*, but as the couples around them prepared for the first figure, Laetitia snapped, "Take me back to my mother at once, Windham."

Some luck, at last! "Very well, if you prefer it."

"You're making a fool of yourself over that middle Parrish sister," she hissed as they approached Lord and Lady Tremblay. "An utter fool, and over a lady of no consequence at all. You may make as much of a fool of yourself as you wish, Windham," she added, lowering her voice. "But you will not make a fool of *me*."

Well, that was plain enough. He'd just been jilted.

Jilted by the belle of the season, and he felt absolutely nothing at all. The truth was, he didn't care for Lady Laetitia Tremblay, and he didn't want to marry her.

How curious, that this should only occur to him *now*. That is, he'd never imagined himself to be besotted with her, but neither had he objected when his father insisted upon the match. He'd thought he could tolerate her just as well as he could any other *ton* bride.

But no longer.

A marriage between them would be a disaster, any chance of happiness an utter impossibility. Of course, his father hadn't given a thought to his happiness when he suggested the match, but then, neither had Cass.

Now he'd seen it, it seemed incredible he'd ever thought he could go forward with the match, but perhaps Hattie had been right when she said he'd been punishing himself, and that he didn't believe he deserved happiness.

Wasn't it also true that he no longer knew what happiness looked like? He'd been under his father's thumb for so long he'd forgotten it.

But he'd been happy, once. In Kent, all those years ago, when he'd lay under the beech tree with Hattie. All those years ago, when she'd been his best—his only—friend.

If she hadn't come to London when she had, he would have gone ahead and married Lady Laetitia. If she hadn't come, his life would have gone on much as it had been since he'd become the Earl of Windham.

He would have continued to float on the surface of it, not a part of it but not free of it either. He would have gone on gaming and drinking and brawling until the tidal wave took him at last, the water closing over his head.

The life his father had created for him would have drowned him.

But Hattie *had* come. Not for the Horticultural Society lecture, as she'd claimed, and not to hear Sir Joseph Banks.

Not for the season, either, no matter how much she insisted otherwise.

She'd come for him. How had it taken him so long to realize it?

Hattie had come to London for *him*, because even now, after twelve years of absence and dozens of unanswered letters, she was still the best friend he'd ever had.

He left Laetitia with a frowning Lady Tremblay and went off in search of Hattie, but he didn't find her. He circled the ballroom once, then again, but she was nowhere to be seen.

Eventually he found Hayward near the double doors that led into Lady Dumfries's ballroom, his avid gaze following Lady Sarah as she took to the floor with Lord Eustace.

"Where the devil is Lady Harriet, Hayward?" He paced to one side of the double doors, turned on his heel and paced back again. "I don't see her anywhere."

"Perhaps she went to the ladies' retiring room. She can't have gotten far. For God's sake, Windham, will you cease that pacing? All your flailing about is giving me motion sickness."

Cass snapped his pocket watch closed and stuffed it into the pocket of his spotless black Weston coat. Watching the tiny gold hand ticking off the passing of each minute was driving him mad. "She's been gone for nearly half an hour."

"Perhaps she's dancing again. Who can tell, in this crush?"

"I despise balls." The ballroom was far too hot, and the entire company was stuffed together cheek to jowl, and there wasn't a breath of fresh air to be had. One young lady had already succumbed to a swoon.

"Everyone despises balls. The gentlemen, anyway. But I shouldn't worry, Windham. Lady Harriet will turn up."

He'd hoped to have a word with her before the dancing began, to warn her once again to be on her guard with Egerton, but Lady Fosberry had arrived rather late, and God knew if Laetitia had been obliged to sit out even the first half dozen notes of the opening waltz the tantrum that would have followed would shake London's foundations.

The belle of the season must not be made a wallflower, not even for a matter of seconds. In any case, he was meant to be a gentleman, and a gentleman didn't leave his partner waiting, no matter how disagreeable he found her.

He had to see Hattie and tell her...tell her that he...damn it, he hadn't any idea what he needed to tell her, yet it was surging like a tidal wave inside him all the same, and holding it back was like trying to contain the ocean in his clenched fists.

He searched the ballroom for a flutter of a blue gown, but there were too many bodies surging this way and that, and all of them too close together—

"Windham." Hayward nudged him and nodded toward the door. "On the other side of the ballroom."

There, near the gilt chairs placed around the perimeter of the ballroom were the Parrish sisters, and with them Lady Fosberry, who was so overflowing with satisfaction she looked like a cat who'd just devoured a bowl of cream.

Her three charges were, by every measure, a stunning success, and she knew it.

They all looked breathtaking. Sarah was as sweet and fresh as a rose in a pale pink silk gown, and Margaret wore a flattering primrose gown that put him in mind of the splash of yellow tucked between the frothy white petals of a summer daisy.

But there wasn't a lady in the ballroom who was as breathtaking as Hattie.

Laetitia had been right about one thing. That was no ordinary Celestial blue she was wearing. This was a blue both darker than Celestial blue and brighter than it at once, a deeply saturated, eye-catching blue that verged on purple without quite going over the edge.

It wasn't a shade of blue one often saw on a young lady, and certainly not a lady attending her first London ball. It was too dramatic for that, too bold to be strictly appropriate, but she was so lovely in it, so utterly resplendent it was as if the vibrant color had been created especially for her.

She hadn't worn the purple ostrich feathers. She hadn't worn any feathers at all, and the smooth, pale skin of her bosom was bare of jewels. Her only decoration was a narrow, blue silk ribbon around her neck. A modest headband with a blue silk flower that matched her gown held back a thick cascade of fair curls. Her white silk gloves were tight to the elbow, and tiny, sparking sapphires dangled from her ears.

He forgot about the Sussex Waltz. He forgot about Egerton and Lady Laetitia, and the purple ostrich feathers he and Hattie had laughed about at *Le Maison des Dames*.

The ballroom around them faded away as he approached her, her face all he could see. Hayward said something to him as he stepped forward to take Hattie's hand, but he didn't hear it.

It didn't matter. Nothing mattered but her.

"If you'll pardon me, Windham, I claimed Lady Harriet's first *two* dances." Egerton stepped smoothly in front of him, a smirk on his lips. "This is my dance."

"Easy there, Windham," Hayward murmured as Egerton took Hattie's arm with a proprietary air that made Cass's hands clench into fists.

"I don't like the familiar way he's touching her, Hayward."

"No, I don't care for it either." Hayward's voice was tight with anger. "But there's nothing you can do about it. You'll only hurt Lady Harriet if you make a scene. Keep your wits about you, Windham."

They stood there for some time watching the dancers move through a quadrille, which proved to be as endless as the Sussex Waltz had. At last, the music ended, but Egerton didn't return Hattie to Lady Fosberry.

Cass waited, scanning the crowd, but he didn't see Hattie, and still she and Egerton didn't come. Where could he have taken her?

"What's the matter, Windham?" Hayward nudged him. "You look as if you've seen a ghost."

"The dance has ended, and Hattie hasn't yet returned. Do you see her?"

"No. There are too many people. I can't see a thing." Hayward frowned. "You don't think he'd take her off somewhere, do you?"

"Yes, I do. Go around to the left, and I'll take the right, and we'll meet back here. Make haste, Hayward."

Cass shot off in the other direction, weaving his way through what felt like thousands of people, searching for a flash of golden curls or the flutter of a deep blue gown. Lady Dumfries's ballroom felt enormous as he hurried around the perimeter, ignoring greetings as he went, his throat closing in rage and panic with every step.

Where was she? Had Egerton taken her somewhere? Hattie knew better than to disappear with Egerton, but if he had managed to lure her away, or worse, forced her, it could be hours before they were found.

By that time, Hattie's reputation would be ruined. It was, doubtless, precisely what Egerton wanted to happen. If the *ton* believed Egerton had compromised Hattie, a marriage between them would be the only way to save her reputation. He wouldn't put it past Egerton to intentionally compromise her. It was the surest way to get a hold of her money.

This was his fault. He should never have befriended Egerton in the first place. He'd known who and what Egerton was, but he'd allowed the man into his home anyway. If he'd had even a shred of self-respect, Egerton would not have been in his townhouse at all, and he never would have seen Hattie's letters.

By the time he met up with Hayward again he was breathless, either from running around the ballroom, or rage. He couldn't have said which. "Did you see her, Hayward?"

"No, and not Egerton, either. They both seem to have vanished. This is bad, Windham."

It was. It was as bad as it could be.

"Let Lady Fosberry know, would you, Hayward? It's possible Hattie isn't missing at all and simply went to the ladies' retiring room. Lady Fosberry will know if that's the case."

But it wasn't. He couldn't have said how he knew, but he did.

"Yes, right away."

Hayward rushed off toward Lady Fosberry, and Cass flew out the ballroom door, but as soon as he reached the corridor he stopped. Where should he start? Lady Dumfries's townhouse was three floors, with endless nooks and crannies and dark corridors, and that was to say nothing of the garden.

And Hattie had disappeared without a trace.

CHAPTER

ELEVEN

I t had been a mistake, accepting Lord Egerton's invitation to dance.

Not just one dance, either, but *two*. That tedious Sussex Waltz, followed by an equally tedious quadrille. Whatever madness had made her agree to such torture, she heartily regretted it now.

It wasn't that she could complain about Lord Egerton's manners. He'd asked her a great many questions, perhaps more questions than was strictly polite, but otherwise he'd behaved as respectfully as any young lady could possibly demand.

"I believe this is the first ball you've attended in London, is it not, Lady Harriet?"

"Yes, my lord."

They were separated by the figures of the dance before she could say more, but Lord Egerton resumed his interrogation as soon as they were joined again. "Your first season, as well?

My, he was curious, wasn't he? "Yes, my lord."

"Your family doesn't often venture out of Kent, then?" Lord Egerton's hand pressed more firmly against her back. "I understand that your brother Lord Melrose has not yet arrived in London?"

"No, my lord." His hand was too warm. She could feel a trace of dampness on his palm even through the silk of his gloves, and it was all she could do not to flinch away from him. "He has business that is keeping him in Oxfordshire at the moment."

"Ah, I see. Do you expect him soon?"

It was the third time he'd questioned her about Johnathan, and his relentless quizzing was growing wearying. "The date of his and Lady Melrose's arrival has not yet been determined, my lord."

"Ah. And so, the three lovely young Parrish sisters are left all alone in London."

"Alone?" What an odd thing to say. "We're hardly alone, Lord Egerton. We have Lady Fosberry."

"Of course, of course." He smiled at her. "I beg your pardon, Lady Harriet."

She didn't quite like that smile, somehow. There was something...*knowing* about it, as if he knew something she did not.

But perhaps she wasn't being fair to Lord Egerton. He hadn't done anything wrong, exactly, yet Cass's voice kept echoing in her head, warning her against the man, and urging her to keep away from him.

He's neither respectable, nor a gentleman...

Lord Egerton made her uneasy, but it was no small thing

to question a gentleman's respectability, and she didn't like to jump to conclusions.

But despite the recent turmoil between her and Cass, she couldn't find it in herself to doubt him. There were a great many unanswered questions and misunderstandings between them, but Cass would never lie to her.

In the end, it all ruined her enjoyment in her first two dances at a London ball. She spent the duration of it peering over Lord Egerton's shoulder toward the corner of the ballroom Lady Fosberry had commandeered and envying the young ladies who'd been condemned to sit out the first dance for lack of a partner.

How much simpler it must be to be a wallflower!

By the time the musicians played the last note of *Le Pantalon*, it was everything she could do not to flee the ballroom altogether and spend the rest of the evening hiding in the ladies' retiring room.

"I thank you for the pleasure of your company, my lord." She offered Lord Egerton a hasty curtsey and began to back away from him. "If you'll pardon me, I believe Lady Fosberry is looking for me."

He stopped her with a hand on her arm. "I shall deliver you to her forthwith, Lady Harriet. Shall we skirt around the perimeter of the ballroom? It will be much quicker if we avoid the crush."

In the interest of shedding Lord Egerton more quickly than not, she gave a distracted nod and let him guide her through the press of bodies, but somehow she lost sight of Lady Fosberry entirely as they weaved this way and that, and the first inklings of uneasiness tripped down her spine.

But no, she was being ridiculous. They were in the middle of a crowded ballroom, for pity's sake, with hundreds of people surrounding them. Even if Lord Egerton was every bit the villain Cass claimed he was, he wouldn't dare try and—

"You look overly warm, Lady Harriet. Perhaps I'd better take you for a breath of air. I'd never forgive myself if you succumbed to a swoon."

"I'm not at all warm, my lord, and I don't have the least intention of—"

"A mere breath, Lady Harriet."

"That's not necessary, my lord. I'm perfectly well."

"Nonsense, my lady. Your cheeks are terribly flushed."

"Lord Egerton!" She stopped, tugging at her arm. "I must insist you release me at once."

But Lord Egerton didn't release her. He tightened his grip, his fingers digging into her flesh as he all but dragged her toward a shallow alcove set into an overlooked corner of the ballroom.

This time, real alarm shot through her. "Let go of me!"

She managed to tear her arm free of his hold, but with the quickness of a snake snatching its prey he seized her wrist in a punishing grip. "Not so fast, Lady Harriet."

He yanked her forward with such violence she tripped, and one of her slippers came off her foot, but he paid it no mind and kept pulling her toward a door set into the back wall of the alcove.

It wasn't a door one was likely to stumble across accidentally. It was set well away from the main part of the ballroom, but Lord Egerton had certainly known it was there, and—

Dear God. He'd planned this! That was why he'd solicited her hand for the first two dances. He'd intended to get her alone from the start, and he couldn't have chosen a better place for it. There was no one nearby. The alcove was dimly lit, and far enough away from the rest of the company that she could only just make out the murmur of the crowd and the faint strains of a violin playing another country dance.

Panic swept over her, and she began to struggle in earnest. "Release me! How dare you? Lord Egerton, I insist you—"

"Be quiet, Lady Harriet."

By this point they'd reached the door, and he jerked it open with one hand and attempted to force her through it with his body, but fear gave her a strength she hadn't realized she possessed, and she slammed her foot down on top of his. It might have been enough to make him release her if she hadn't lost her slipper, but alas, a kick with a bare foot had little effect, and he merely laughed.

Rage and panic fogged her brain, and before she knew what she was about, she'd sunk her fingernails into his wrist, just above the edge of his glove where the silk gave way to bare skin.

"Damn it!" He jerked his hand away and stared down at the smear of blood seeping from the cut she'd left. "You've ruined my glove, you ridiculous chit! You'll pay for your insolence once we're married!"

Married? What in the world did he mean? "You're mad! I'm not going to marry you!"

He yanked her through the door, slammed it shut behind them and pushed her against it, pinning her there with his body. "Oh, but you will, my lady. You may be certain of that."

A chilly wind sliced through her and goosebumps rose on the bare skin of her neck and shoulders. Were they outdoors? She cast a quick glance around her, trying to get her bearings.

They'd come out on some sort of terrace with a wrought iron railing surrounding it, and what looked like a small garden underneath it.

If she could manage to get over the side of the railing—

"Before you do anything foolish, Lady Harriet, may I remind you Lady Dumfries's ballroom is on the second floor of her townhouse." He waved a hand toward the railing, a smirk on his lips. "I daresay you could get over it, but you'll find it's a long way down."

She stared at him, fear clawing at her and stealing her reason. Oh, why hadn't she listened to Cass! He'd been right about Lord Egerton all along, and like a fool, she'd dismissed his warnings.

Now it was too late. He had her just where he wanted her.

But if Lord Egerton thought she'd dissolve into floods of tears, he was very much mistaken. She wouldn't give in so easily as that.

She clenched her hands into fists to keep them from shaking and raised her chin. "I don't know what you hope to accomplish with this disgraceful stunt, Lord Egerton. I will not marry you. I wouldn't marry you if you were the only gentleman left in England."

He threw his head back in a laugh. "Such spirit! But that's where you're wrong, Lady Harriet. You will indeed marry me, if you value your reputation."

"Ah, I understand it now. You think to keep me out here long enough for the *ton* to draw all the wrong conclusions. But you've chosen the wrong lady for your games, my lord. My brother will never force me into a marriage I don't want, no matter if the *ton* does believe I've been compromised. You may as well let me return to Lady Fosberry."

She attempted to step away from him, but he blocked her and thrust his face into hers, so close she could taste the stench of his breath. He was panting with exertion, a thin sheen of sweat covering his face. Bile rushed into her throat, and it was all she could do not to gag.

"No, I don't think so, Lady Harriet. But you've quite mistaken the matter, you know. I have no intention of compromising you, although I admit it's tempting." He caught one of her ringlets in his hand, laughing when she jerked away from him. "This is about your letters."

Letters? What letters? He truly had gone mad. "I have no idea what you're—"

"Your letters to Lord Windham, Lady Harriet. Or should I call you Hattie?"

Her letters to Cass? She stared up at him, frozen in shock.

No. No, it was impossible. Cass would never hurt her by showing her letters to a blackguard like Lord Egerton. He'd never show them to anyone.

But if Cass hadn't told him, how could Lord Egerton possibly know about—

"Twelve years' worth of letters, I believe. Yes, Lord

Windham told me all about it. He said you continued to write to him even after he gave up the correspondence." Lord Egerton tutted. "Rather humiliating for you, really. But of course, the damage was already done by then."

No, it wasn't true. She opened her mouth to argue, to scream, to rail at Lord Egerton until he took it all back, every word of it, but all that emerged was a broken sob.

Lord Egerton saw his advantage and ruthlessly seized it. "I wonder what your brother will make of twelve years' of such flagrant disobedience on your part, Lady Harriet? Rather shocking, isn't it?"

"My brother would never—"

"You going missing from the ballroom is more than enough to ruin you, but there are your sisters to think about, as well. I should think your illicit correspondence with Lord Windham combined with your shocking lapse of propriety this evening is more than enough to ruin all three of you."

Margaret and Sarah, ruined? Margaret, who was almost certainly in love with Lord Hayward, and Sarah who'd only just begun living her life after so many years of illness...

How would she ever forgive herself if they were ruined because of her carelessness? It had been *her* idea to come to London, *her* idea not to mention it to Johnathan. It had been *her* who'd told Cass they'd come for the season, and she still hadn't told him the truth.

She'd lied to everybody. Her brother, Cass, her sisters, and Lady Fosberry.

And now she was at the mercy of a reprobate like Lord Egerton, because this was what came of keeping secrets and telling lies.

"You look distressed, Lady Harriet, but there's really no need to be. I'm willing to marry you, despite your damaged reputation." He pressed closer, looming over her until she shrank back against the door. "Now listen carefully, my lady. You're going to tell your brother it's a love match between us."

"I will do no such—"

"Indeed, you will, or I'll see to it your sisters leave London in a cloud of infamy. We'll marry, and your sisters' reputations will remain as spotless as ever. As for you, I promise you I'll be an ardent husband."

She turned her face away from the drift of his hot breath against her cheek, but he caught her chin in a rough grip, his eyes glittering. "Come, my lady. Haven't you even one kiss for your betrothed?"

It was no use fighting him. He was too strong, and there was no place to escape to, no place to go. She went blank as he lowered his mouth to hers, the terrace and the railing and Lord Egerton's hated face all went blurry as his mouth came closer and closer—

All at once the door she'd been pinned against jerked open. She toppled backwards and would have fallen, but before she hit the floor a pair of warm, strong arms closed around her, and she was caught against a solid, muscular chest.

The deep rumble of a familiar voice penetrated the haze around her, hoarse and ragged with rage. "Take a step toward me, Egerton. I dare you."

❧

CASS KNEW WHAT ANGER WAS. He'd been angry at his father for as long as he could remember, but the fury pouring through him now was unlike anything he'd ever experienced before.

His blood burned with such rage it felt as if flames were roaring through his veins.

If Egerton so much as twitched, he was going to tear him limb from limb.

"Now, Windham. There's no need to fly into a temper." Egerton was backing away, his hands held out in front of him. "Hattie and I were just having a little chat, that's all."

"Hattie? Did you just say *Hattie*, Egerton?" Her childhood nickname on this vile scoundrel's lips lit a spark inside Cass that was destined to burst into a conflagration. "You don't call her Hattie, Egerton. *Not ever*. Do you understand me?"

"Yes, yes, of course. I beg your pardon, Windham." Egerton backed away until he came up against the iron railing and could go no further. "I wasn't going to hurt her. I was just—"

"Yes, you were." There was only one reason a villain like Egerton absconded from the ballroom with an innocent lady and brought her to a dark, abandoned terrace. "You dragged her here because you meant to hurt her."

Hattie hadn't gone with Egerton willingly. A besotted lady sneaking off for a passionate interlude with a favored gentleman didn't leave her slipper behind.

She felt so small against him, her slender bones so fragile, and she was shaking, violent tremors wracking her body. Whatever Egerton had done to her, it had badly frightened her.

Gently, he eased her away from him. "Go back to Lady Fosberry now, Hattie."

She gazed up at him, her eyes two enormous indistinct smudges in her pale face. "I—I don't want to leave without you."

"It's all right. Lady Fosberry and your sisters are looking for you. Go on."

It nearly killed him to send her away alone, but Lady Fosberry was already beside herself with worry, and it was best if Hattie didn't witness what he was about to do to Egerton.

She clutched at the lapels of his coat. "He knows about the letters, Cass."

He'd guessed as much. He couldn't say how Egerton had found out Hattie was the one who'd sent them, but he'd know the whole of it before he left this terrace, no matter if he had to beat the truth out of Egerton.

Now wasn't the time to discuss it, however. "I know. It's all right." He pressed a quick kiss to her forehead, then helped her out the door, waiting to make sure she'd reached the corridor before he closed it with a soft click.

Only then did he turn to Egerton.

"Now, Windham, be reasonable. We're old friends, are we not? There's no reason to—"

He broke off with a strangled whimper as Cass advanced on him, seized him by his coat and shook him until Egerton's teeth rattled inside his head.

"We're not friends, Egerton. We never were, and I should have done this the first time you touched those letters."

Egerton drew himself up with the only shreds of dignity

left to a man who was seconds away from a beating. "Of course, a St. Giles guttersnipe like you would resort to violence. You're no gentleman, Windham—oof!"

Cass put all his strength into the blow to Egerton's jaw. There was a sickly crunch as Egerton's head snapped back. His legs gave out underneath him and he dropped to the floor, his body going as limp as a ragdoll.

Cass crouched down beside him. "How did you find out Lady Harriet is the Hattie from my letters, Egerton?"

It wasn't likely Egerton had guessed it. Hattie was a unique nickname, and not one of the usual derivatives of the name Harriet. Lady Fosberry and Hattie's sisters referred to Hattie by the nickname occasionally, but not usually in formal company.

Someone must have told Egerton, but who?

"I don't have to tell you a damned thing, Windham." Egerton pressed his gloved fingers to his mouth, where a thin trickle of blood was seeping from the corner of his lip. "Bloody savage."

"Very well then, Egerton. Have it your way." He drew his arm back again, but Egerton, being the coward he was, shrank back with a whimper. "All right! Jesus, Windham. Lady Laetitia told me."

Lady Laetitia? How the devil could Lady Laetitia possibly have found out that—

Wait. Had he used Hattie's nickname when he'd been speaking to her at *Le Maison des Dames*?

Lady Laetitia had been there that day, too. She'd come upon them seemingly out of nowhere when he and Hattie had been discussing Lord Melrose's continued absence from London.

He must have called her Hattie that day, and Laetitia, with the uncanny knack she had for gossip and maliciousness had been in just the right place to overhear it.

Laetitia had learned Hattie's nickname from *him*.

Of course, she'd told Egerton. Laetitia wasn't one to let such a tasty morsel of gossip slip by her. She'd known just who to bring it to, and Egerton, who despised him, must have been only too delighted to hear it.

Egerton had been seeking revenge against him ever since he'd ended their friendship over the letters. What better way to get back at him, and at the same time win himself a wealthy bride? God knew Egerton was never going to have one of Lord Melrose's younger sisters otherwise.

Egerton must have told Laetitia that Cass was writing to someone named Hattie. Laetitia had put the whole of it together that day at Madame Céline's, and between the two of them they'd concluded that the mysterious Hattie who'd sent him all those affectionate letters was none other than Lady Harriet Parrish.

So, Egerton had made his plans, and now he was going to pay for them.

"Listen to me, Egerton, and listen well. If I find out you've breathed a single word against Lady Harriet, or impugned her reputation in any way, it won't just be your jaw next time. It will be your neck."

Egerton stared up at him with bleary eyes. His jaw was already swelling, and a large red mark that promised to turn black and blue within hours was blooming on his cheek.

"Look at me, Egerton. Do we understand each other? Not a single, bloody word."

Egerton nodded, his eyes wide.

"Say it."

"Not a word against Lady Harriet, or it's my neck."

"Very good, Egerton. That wasn't so hard, was it?"

"I wish you success with Lady Harriet, Windham." Egerton spat out a mouthful of blood. "She's under the impression it was you who told me about her letters."

"Now where would she get that idea, Egerton?" As if he didn't know.

Blood gushed from Egerton's mouth as his lips split in a ghastly grin. "I told her so."

Of course, he had.

"You know, Egerton, for all that blood pouring down your chin, you don't appear properly chastised for your reprehensible behavior. In the interests of making sure we thoroughly understand each other..." He caught Egerton's coat in his clenched fists, and with one violent wrench, thumped Egerton's head against the wrought iron railing behind him.

It wasn't enough. Egerton deserved so much worse, but even a St. Giles guttersnipe drew the line at murdering a peer at Lady Dumfries's ball.

If only just.

He rose to his feet and slipped out the door without a backward glance, leaving Egerton lying in a boneless heap behind him.

Egerton would find his way out eventually. Or not.

Cass didn't give a damn, either way.

TWELVE

B y the time Cass returned to the ballroom Hattie, her sisters and Lady Fosberry were gone. It was just as well, as the evening's scandal was already making its way from every mouth to every ear.

And it had already made it to Hayward's ear, judging by his grim expression.

As soon as Hayward saw him approaching he signaled to Cass to follow him, turned on his heel and left the ballroom. He didn't say a word as they waited for Hayward's carriage to be brought, and the ride from Lady Dumfries's ball to Cass's townhouse in Mount Street also passed in utter silence.

Neither of them moved when Massey stopped the carriage outside Cass's townhouse in Mount Street. Hayward sat in one corner of the carriage, his every appendage stiff in a silent mutiny, his knees locked together, and his arms crossed over his chest. If he could have crossed his upper and lower lip he certainly would have, but instead he settled for pinching them tightly together.

It wasn't the first time Hayward had been angry with him. He'd been subjected to Hayward's pinched-lipped glare on any number of occasions. Hayward had his own private sense of proper behavior, despite his mildly rakish tendencies. In his friend's estimation, there were certain things a gentleman simply did not *do*.

Brawling at a private ball was one of them.

Cass's own moral code was a touch flimsier than Hayward's, and so he'd never troubled himself much with his friend's fits and tempers. They'd always had an unspoken agreement that Hayward was welcome to disapprove of him, and Cass was welcome to ignore that disapproval.

But this time he couldn't abide his friend's seething discontent.

This time, it was different. This time, it wasn't his gaming, or his drunkenness, or his tendency to dally with a lady he'd much better not have dallied with that had earned him Hayward's ire.

Yes, he'd engaged in a brawl at a ball, and half of Lady Dumfries's guests had witnessed Egerton stumbling into the ballroom looking as if he'd been trampled by a horse.

By tomorrow morning, all of London would know of it.

Was it his finest moment? No. But this time, for the first time since he'd come to London, Cass *wasn't* ashamed of his behavior. Egerton had *hurt* Hattie. The man was a villain, and it was well past time someone held him to account for it.

Still, he wasn't immune to Hayward's silence, and he'd rather have it out between them sooner than later. "I sense a lecture in the making, Hayward. You may as well get it over with."

Hayward raised an eyebrow but stubbornly maintained his stoic silence.

"At least the gossips will be pleased with me. I daresay the scandal sheets will enjoy a brisk business tomorrow morning. The *ton* does love a brawl."

Hayward glared at him, but his lips remained closed.

"Nothing at all to say, Hayward? No sermons or speeches? No treatise on the proper way for a gentleman to conduct himself? That *is* unusual. I expected a reprimand, at least."

Nothing. Not even a sternly raised eyebrow.

Cass sighed. "Very well, Hayward. Massey will take you on to the Albany. Massey, if you'd be so good as to take Lord Hayward on to Piccadilly—"

"If you'd be so good as to wait here for me, Massey," Hayward interrupted. "Lord Windham and I are going to have a chat first. I won't be long."

That was a bald-faced lie. Hayward had never delivered a short lecture in his life.

Exhaustion was catching up to Cass, a heavy weariness seeping through the cracks, and he wanted his bed more than anything, but there was no arguing with Hayward's grim tone. Even if he'd had a mind to, Hayward was already out of the carriage and striding up the steps to the front door, and there was little he could do but accept his fate and trail after his friend to his study.

His moment of reckoning had come at last. A bit overdue, really, all told.

Hayward didn't bother to light a lamp but went directly to the sideboard and helped himself to a splash of brandy. He drank it down quickly, then poured two more, and handed one to Cass before planting himself in front of the fireplace.

He still didn't speak but stood there as silent as a cipher and as stiff as the fireplace pokers in the rack beside him, his stern gaze fixed on Cass.

Ah. So, they were back to seething disapproval, then.

For God's sake, why didn't Hayward say something? Cass squirmed as the silence stretched between them, until he could stand it no longer and snapped, "Well, Hayward? You've clearly got something to say, so you may as well say it, and put us both out of our misery."

"Very well, Windham, since you insist." Hayward tossed back his brandy, placed the empty glass on the mantel, then turned to face Cass. "Would you care to explain what happened with Egerton? Because from what I can see it looks as if you made an utter cake of yourself tonight."

Heat rose in Cass's cheeks, but it wasn't shame. Not this time. It was anger. "I'm aware of how it looks, Hayward, but—"

"Are you, Windham? Are you truly aware? Tell me, did you see Lady Dumfries's face when she realized what had happened in her ballroom?"

"It happened on the terrace, not in the ballroom."

"Splitting hairs, Windham."

"I didn't see Lady Dumfries's face, no. You'll have to excuse me, Hayward. I was a bit preoccupied with planting my fist in Egerton's jaw at the time."

"Well, I did see her face. Nearly everyone in the ballroom saw it, and you may be sure it's all anyone will be talking about as they pay their calls tomorrow. By this time tomorrow evening, all of London will know of it."

"I don't give a damn what the *ton* says."

"That's precisely my point, Windham! You can't simply do whatever you—"

"Egerton's a brute. He got what he deserved."

"Egerton's a brute, so you deemed it appropriate to brawl with him in the middle of Lady Dumfries's ball?"

"Can it properly be called a brawl? I struck Egerton, and Egerton toppled over like a nine pin. It was hardly a brawl." He didn't mention that he'd also slammed Egerton's head against the wrought iron gate, as it didn't seem likely to help matters.

But he didn't regret it. Perhaps he would later, but not now. There'd be plenty of time for self-recrimination when he was alone in his bed.

"Are you entertained, Windham. Is this amusing to you?"

"Amusing, to find the lady I lo...a lady I care very much for suffering such an insult by a scoundrel like Egerton? He was hurting Hattie, Hayward."

"*What?*" Hayward whispered, the color draining from his face.

"He was hurting her." Cass clutched his glass tighter to keep himself from hurling it into the grate and watching it shatter into a thousand shards. "Egerton was...he tried to hurt Hattie, Hayward. What would you have had me do?"

"Dear God, Windham." Hayward reached for the arm of a chair to steady himself and sank into it. "I had no idea."

Cass leaped to his feet, unable to sit still a moment longer. "God, Hayward, Hattie's face! I won't soon forget her expression when I burst onto the terrace and found her pinned against the door with Egerton looming over her. She was utterly terrified."

"I sincerely beg your pardon, Windham. I should have known better than to trust the rumors flying around the ballroom. The gossips always paint you as the villain."

"The *ton* already has their own version of events, then?" It didn't surprise him. They always did, and he'd been the villain often enough to give any lie the appearance of truth.

He was, after all, a St. Giles guttersnipe, and this was not his first brawl.

"They have it that you attacked Egerton in a hallway outside the ballroom and threatened to throw him from the second floor of Lady Dumfries's townhouse."

"I should have done just that, since I'm to be blamed for it anyway." It was no wonder Egerton had returned to the ballroom after their encounter. What better way to start that rumor than to appear in public bloodied and battered?

"I knew Egerton was a villain, but this?" Hayward shook his head. "How did he discover that Lady Harriet and Hattie were one and the same person?"

"It's a long story, but the short version is that Lady Laetitia Tremblay told him."

"I might have known. That woman is pure poison. You're well rid of her." Hayward glanced at him, eyebrow raised. "You *are* rid of her, are you not?"

"God, yes, and I hope my father is rolling in his grave right now. I hope he never has a moment of peaceful rest again."

"It's wicked to wish ill on the dead, but in your father's

case, I'll make an exception." Hayward hesitated. "Is Lady Harriet going to be all right?"

"I don't know." Cass dragged his hand down his face. "I don't know, Hayward. She was badly shaken."

Sweet, gentle Hattie, who'd never hurt a soul had been utterly at Egerton's mercy tonight. He'd relive her terror again and again, but the part of tonight's disaster that kept playing over in his mind, the part that would keep him up tonight was the question of what might have happened if he hadn't reached her when he did.

What if she hadn't lost her slipper, and he hadn't been able to find her? What if he'd arrived five minutes later than he had? Or ten? God above, but he couldn't bear to think of it.

"Egerton got what he deserved, Hayward. He's villain and shouldn't be tolerated in decent society."

But the *ton* had never been particularly discriminating when it came to aristocratic gentlemen, particularly those with money. They'd tolerated his father, hadn't they?

They'd tolerated *him*.

"I don't dispute it, Windham. Only the worst sort of monster would hurt a lady."

Cass threw himself back into his chair, suddenly drained. "What do you think would have happened if I hadn't found her when I did, Hayward?"

The very thought of what that blackguard might have done to Hattie made his stomach roil with rage and fear, but he kept his grip on his glass, because throwing it into the grate was too much like something his father would have done.

"You'll drive yourself mad with that question, Windham.

Best not to ask it at all. You did find her, and that's what matters."

Cass said nothing, only stared into his glass, avoiding his friend's eyes.

"I don't blame you for any of this, Windham. You did what you had to do. I only wish it hadn't happened in the middle of Lady Dumfries's ballroom. There's bound to be a scandal now, and you and Lady Harriet will be blamed for the incident far more than Egerton will."

It was the truth. They would be blamed, and there wasn't a damn thing he could do to protect Hattie from the gossips' vicious tongues now. "If there'd been any way to handle it more discreetly, I would have, for her sake."

"I know, Windham. You weren't the villain tonight. Egerton was."

"Yes, well, I hardly see myself as the hero in this scenario. Don't think I don't know that there's very little difference between me and Egerton."

Hayward stared at him. "For God's sake, Windham, you're nothing like Egerton!"

Cass startled at the shock in Hayward's voice. "That was a point on which I thought we'd agree."

"Are you mad? Of course, I don't agree. Egerton is a lying, fortune-hunting, black-hearted scoundrel. Do you think I'd call a man like that my friend?"

"I...no? I never thought of it that way before." Cass cleared the lump from his throat. "But I don't—"

Hayward held up his hand. "You have your irregularities, Windham, but you're hardly a monster. You're just a trifle misguided, and no wonder, with the father you had."

"Misguided?" Cass laughed, but it was an ugly, broken sound. "I'm my father's son, Hayward."

Hayward didn't reply right away. Cass held his breath as his friend sat staring into the dying fire, the pale orange light flickering over his face, until finally, Hayward turned to face him. "That's pure bollocks, Windham."

"How is it bollocks? I'm a Windham, Hayward, and if that isn't bad enough, before I was a Windham I was a St. Giles guttersnipe. There isn't a drop of worthy blood inside me."

Hayward shook his head. "Those are your father's words, not yours."

"They're both of our words. I'm just like—"

"Stop it, Windham! For God's sake, do you suppose your father would have gone to look for Lady Harriet tonight? Do you think he would have protected her as you did? He would have let Egerton drag her away and never given it a second thought. That's what your father would have done. The man had no conscience. But you do. You always have."

Was that true? God, he didn't know. He didn't know anything anymore, except that he'd tried to do the right thing by Hattie when he'd cut off their correspondence. He'd been so sure it would be better for her to be rid of him, and yet...

Would he ever be able to stay away from Hattie? She'd been a part of him for as long as he could remember, the best part of him. Ending their friendship was like an amputation, as if he'd ripped his still beating heart from his chest.

"Listen to me, Windham, and try and get this through your thick skull, will you? If you were anything like your father, you never would have fallen in love with Lady Harriet at all. He didn't have the first idea what love was, but you... well, you've made a bloody mess of it, that's certain, but that's what gentlemen do when they fall in love. They make a mess of things."

He'd certainly done that, hadn't he? Although he'd had some help in that regard.

"Hattie thinks I'm the one who told Egerton about the letters she wrote to me."

Hayward rolled his eyes. "Let me guess. Egerton told her that?"

"Yes. What if she despises me now? What if she believes it's true, and never forgives me, Hayward?"

"Lady Harriet is far too clever to be taken in by Egerton's lies. If you don't believe me, Windham, ask her yourself. You'll see."

Cass grasped this slender thread of hope and held onto it with everything he had, because if she did despise him, and wouldn't forgive him, what would become of him, then?

Even now, months after he'd tried to banish Hattie from his mind and his heart, he could still hear her voice in his head. Everywhere he went, everything he did, she was there with him.

He could see her still as she'd been on the first day, when he'd spied on her through the branches of the beech tree. A fair-haired sprite wearing a crown of wildflowers on her head, her lips curved in a smile as she made daisy chains for her sisters.

For them, and for him. She'd *seen* him that first day, and every day since.

All he'd ever wanted to do was protect her. From villains

like Egerton, and from the *ton*, with their vicious, wagging tongues.

But most of all, he'd wanted to protect her from himself. From the wicked Earl of Windham, a wicked son, born to a wicked father.

Yet there was a single, fundamental truth behind all his arguments and doubts and excuses, and now he'd given it free reign it was swelling inside him, and it would not stop, it would not be contained. It rose and surged and grew until it was too powerful for him to ignore it any longer.

The truth was there, waiting. It always had been. One way or another, the truth will out.

He'd loved her since the first day he'd laid eyes on her in her brother's meadow. Not romantically at first—they'd been far too young for that then—but for as long as he'd known her, there'd been a part of his heart that belonged to her alone.

He'd loved her before he even understood what love was.

There'd never been anyone for him but Hattie. Why had he fought against it for so long?

She was *his*. She'd always been his, just as he'd always been hers.

He'd waited twelve years for Hattie, and he'd wait the rest of his lifetime for her if he had to, but maybe, just maybe he wouldn't have to.

"You've gone mysteriously quiet, Windham. Have I gotten through to you at last, or are you about to regale me with tales of your imagined wickedness?"

Cass turned to his friend, and a rush of gratitude swept

through him. "You're a good friend, Hayward. The best of friends."

"Of course, I am. That's never been in question." Hayward rose to his feet with a mighty yawn and stretched his arms over his head. "Now that's settled, I'll see myself out, shall I? No doubt poor Massey is ready for his bed."

Cass followed Hayward into the hallway but stopped him at the door. "I'm going to marry her, Hayward. Lady Harriet. I'm going to marry her."

"Are you, indeed? Well done, Windham. A lady like that will be the making of you. But perhaps it can wait until tomorrow? I don't think I can take any more excitement tonight."

THIRTEEN

" I think it's best if I return to Melrose House today."

There, she'd said it.

As expected, three heads swung toward her as the words left her mouth, and Sarah dropped her fork with a clatter. Hattie sat quietly, the eggs she'd been pushing around her plate for the last half hour in front of her, her hands folded neatly in her lap and waited for a storm of protests to break over her head like a thundercloud.

That Margaret, Sarah and Lady Fosberry *would* protest went without saying.

Margaret would remind her it had been her idea to come to London in the first place, and that they'd risked rather a lot to carry out her plan. Sarah, who was no coward, and had never been one to give way in a battle would insist they face the gossiping *ton* head on, and as for Lady Fosberry...

She'd be the most disappointed of all except for Hattie herself, who was so ashamed of her own cowardice she couldn't meet her ladyship's eyes.

It was a bitter pill indeed to have made it so far and overcome so much only to scurry back to Kent with her tail between her legs, but surely they weren't surprised? They must see that after the fiasco at Lady Dumfries's ball last night there was no question of her remaining in London.

The moments ticked silently by, one after the next until at last, Lady Fosberry patted her lips with her serviette. "You don't wish to see the Elgin Marbles today?"

"The Elgin Marbles." Lord Egerton had stumbled into the ballroom last night with a river of blood gushing from his mouth, most of the *ton* had labeled Cass a villain and Hattie a shameless liar, and if that weren't enough, Lord Egerton had forever destroyed the joy she'd taken in her lovely Prussian blue gown.

Her first and last ballgown, and it was ruined, just as her hopes were.

All this, and Lady Fosberry was concerned about the Elgin Marbles.

"Yes, dearest." Lady Fosberry gave her a bright smile. "You did say you wanted to see them, did you not?"

"The Horticultural Society's lectures haven't ended yet, either." Margaret set her fork down beside her half-eaten plate of toast. "Indeed, they've scarcely begun. Sir Joseph Banks's Kew Gardens lecture is tomorrow, and I know you wish to hear it."

"It's bound to be a fascinating account, and it may well be his last public lecture," Lady Fosberry added. "It would be a great pity for you to miss it, Hattie."

Sir Joseph, the Elgin Marbles...it was all pure nonsense. "Are we still acting as if we came to London for the lectures?"

Margaret frowned. "What do you mean? Of course we came for the—"

"No, we didn't, Margaret, and you know it as well as I do. I came to London to see Cass, and you came in hopes of meeting Lord Hayward again."

Margaret stared at her, open-mouthed, her cheeks turning scarlet.

Dash it, she shouldn't have said that, or at least she might have said it with a bit more kindness. She'd made an utter mess of things from the moment she set foot in London, and now she'd hurt Margaret's feelings, as well.

But surely there was no point in pretending any longer?

"I beg your pardon, Margaret." She pushed her plate aside with a sigh. It wasn't as if she could choke down a single morsel of food, not with her stomach still in knots from the events of last night. "That was unkind of me."

She dropped her gaze to her plate as another heavy silence fell over the table, and it might have gone on for the whole of eternity if Sarah hadn't broken it by delicately clearing her throat. "I don't care one whit for either the lectures or the Elgin Marbles. I came to London to see if Alice Weatherby was telling the truth about the *ton*'s shocking scandals."

Lady Fosberry chuckled. "Of course you did, dearest, and who can blame you? Those who haven't witnessed the *ton*'s disgraceful antics can hardly credit a word of the gossip until they see it for themselves."

"Well, I daresay you have your answer, Sarah." Despite her misery, a reluctant smile twitched at Hattie's lips. "It turns out Alice was telling the truth."

"Alice is a dear, sweet thing, if a touch featherbrained." Margaret smiled at Sarah to take the sting from her words before she turned her attention back to Hattie. "Are you certain you want to return to Kent now, after we've come so far? I don't deny last night's ball was a bit trying, but we—"

"Trying?" A soiled pair of gloves or a misplaced book were *trying*. "My dear Margaret, last night's ball was an utter disaster."

The whispers and stares when she'd returned to the ballroom after such a prolonged absence, Lady Laetitia's mocking laughter and Lady Tremblay's gloating expression were the stuff of nightmares.

But none of that compared to the expression on Cass's face when he burst onto the terrace and found her out there alone with Lord Egerton. It had been the single worst moment of her life.

What must Cass have thought of her, when he'd come upon her on a darkened terrace with Lord Egerton, particularly when he'd taken such pains to warn her away from the man? At best, he must think she was every bit as naïve and foolish as he'd accused her of being, to allow herself to be lured away by a scoundrel like Egerton.

At worst, he might have believed she'd gone with Egerton willingly.

The thought made her shudder, but even that wasn't what had kept her awake all night, tossing in her bed. No, the worst of it was that the *ton* was putting the entire blame for the incident on Cass. She'd heard the ladies whispering behind their fans as Lady Fosberry had whisked them out of the ballroom last night.

They said that it wasn't Cass's first brawl, and almost certainly wouldn't be his last. They claimed he was dangerous, an unrepentant villain. Those who didn't blame the hereditary Windham wickedness for the incident were quick to point to Cass's childhood spent in the rookeries as the reason for his behavior.

They'd called him low-born. They said it would have been better if he'd remained in St. Giles.

They'd said he might be an earl, but he wasn't a gentleman.

All this, because he'd saved her from something too awful to contemplate.

How could she ever ask his forgiveness for something like that? His reputation was in tatters, and it was all her fault.

Coming to London had been a mistake.

She'd thought so a dozen times since they arrived, but only because she'd believed *she* would be the one who'd end up hurt. All the while she'd been worrying that Cass would reject her—that he'd tell her he'd decided to stop writing to her because he no longer wished to be her friend.

It had never once occurred to her that *he'd* be the one who'd end up hurt.

How selfish she was, how unthinking—

"Here, drink this, dearest. You look a trifle pale this morning." Lady Fosberry refilled Hattie's teacup. "When did you wish to leave for Kent?"

"Today, if possible. This morning, if the thing can be managed."

Margaret exchanged a glance with Lady Fosberry. "So soon as that?"

"Yes." Now she'd made up her mind to go, she couldn't leave London quickly enough. "You and Sarah needn't return with me," she hastened to add. "If Lady Fosberry can spare a servant to accompany me, I'm happy to make the journey alone."

In truth, "happy" might be a bit of an exaggeration. With the memories of last night's awful scene still fresh in her mind, she wondered if she'd ever be happy again.

"I have no objection to your returning home." Margaret cast another cryptic glance at Lady Fosberry. "If you're certain that's what you—"

"Of course, you must go if you wish, Hattie, but alas, I'm afraid I can't accommodate you today, dearest. The, ah...well, you see, it's the carriage. It's broken."

"Broken? But we took it to and from Lady Dumfries's ball last night, did we not?"

"Yes, indeed! We did, but this morning Coombs informed me that one of the, er...the axles is cracked, and the, ah...what do you call them? Oh, yes. The wheels! The wheels are damaged, and the horse's harnesses are in a terrible state. A terrible state, indeed."

"The axle, and the wheels, *and* the harnesses? My goodness. That is unlucky." More like unlikely, but her suspicious glance was met with identical bright smiles from Margaret and Lady Fosberry.

"It's dreadfully unlucky indeed, but Coombs is seeing to it, and I daresay you can leave tomorrow, or perhaps the next day. Will that do, dear?"

It would have to, wouldn't it?

She dredged up a smile from somewhere, but it felt stiff

on her lips. "Of course, my lady. I don't wish to inconvenience you."

"Not at all, my dear child, not at all." Lady Fosberry patted her hand, but her brow was furrowed with worry. "Last night was dreadful, but I have a feeling it will all be fine in the end. We'll soon see you set to rights again."

There was only one thing that would set her right again, and that was to return to Kent. Just the thought of her beloved home made her ache with longing, but she'd be there soon enough, and once she was back, she'd never make the mistake of venturing into London ever again.

"You haven't eaten a bit of your breakfast, Harriet." Lady Fosberry glanced at her untouched plate. "Shall I have the footmen fetch some of those peach tarts you like? I believe cook made some just this morning."

"No, thank you, my lady. I don't have much of an appetite. I didn't sleep well, and my head aches a bit. I believe I'll retire to my bedchamber."

"All right, dear."

Their anxious gazes followed her as she rose from her seat, but none of them ventured a comment, and she let out a breath of relief as she passed from the breakfast parlor into the corridor. She didn't like to worry them, but she couldn't bear to sit there any longer, pretending everything was fine as her heart broke in her chest.

She dragged herself up the staircase, but just as she reached the upper landing one of the downstairs maidservants called out to her. "Lady Harriet, wait! I beg your pardon, but you have a visitor."

A visitor? She hadn't heard the bell, and it was far too

early in the morning to receive calls. Who would be visiting her, anyway? After last night, she would have thought everyone in London would take care to give her a wide berth.

Scandal, after all, could be contagious.

"Give my excuses, won't you, Mary? I'm a trifle under the weather today."

"Yes, my lady, only the gentleman said it was urgent. A matter of life and death, he said."

Life and death? How strange, but it seemed she was to have no peace at all. "Yes, very well, Mary. I'm coming."

She turned and dragged herself back down the stairs, but she hadn't gone a half-dozen steps before she paused, her feet frozen to the step beneath her.

There, standing in the entryway with his hat in his hand, was Cass.

She pressed her hand to her chest, her heart beating a wild tattoo against her palm. She must have made a noise, because his head jerked up, and his gaze met hers, and for an instant time was suspended as they stared at each other.

He looked different this morning. Oh, he was every inch the elegant Earl of Windham in his fashionable cutaway coat an elaborately embroidered silk waistcoat, but his cravat was slightly askew, as if he'd tied it in a hurry. The shadow of a beard darkened his handsome face, and he looked as if he hadn't slept.

"Cass," she whispered, a tremor in her voice, because just looking at him with those shadowy circles under his eyes was breaking her heart. "What are you doing here?"

"I-I beg your pardon for calling so early, Hat—that is, Lady Harriet. I hoped you'd agree to have a word with me."

He waited, turning his hat in his hands, his gaze locked on her face.

Perhaps she should have refused. Perhaps she should have told him it was best for them each to go their separate ways before someone else got hurt. After everything that had happened, there didn't seem to be anything left to say, and yet...

She'd never been able to refuse Cass anything, and she couldn't refuse him now. She couldn't turn him away any more than she could give up breathing. "Mary, please tell Lady Fosberry Lord Windham is here, and that I've joined him for a walk in the rose garden."

"Yes, my lady." Mary cast a wide-eyed glance at Cass before hurrying off in the direction of the breakfast parlor.

Slowly she descended the staircase, her legs shaking with every step, until she was standing in the entryway with Cass, so close she might have reached out and touched him.

Wordlessly, he offered her his arm, and for better or worse, she took it, because she could do nothing else. She would always take Cass's arm, every time he offered it to her.

They didn't speak, and they didn't look at each other, but as he led her through the entryway and out the front door his height and broad shoulders kept the chilly wind at bay, and his arm felt warm and solid beneath her fingertips.

She'd always felt safe with Cass, and despite everything that had happened, she still did.

Surely, that must mean something.

～

AFTER THE LIES Egerton had told her about the letters, Cass had feared Hattie would refuse to see him this morning. Even now, with her small hand on his arm and the soft crunch of her boots on the pathway, he could hardly believe she was here.

Regret had found him last night as soon as his head touched his pillow, just as he'd known it would. One's sins always seemed darker at night than they did in the cold light of day.

He had no misgivings about the brawl with Egerton. If he hadn't been certain another scandal would hurt Hattie, he and Egerton would have been facing each other at dawn this morning.

The villain had gotten less than he deserved.

But where Hattie was concerned, his conscience wasn't as clear as he might have wished.

He should never have left her side at the ball last night. He should have prevented Egerton from dancing with her, he should have kept a better eye on her...the self-recriminations went on and on, the apologies hovering on his lips, but now he had her alone at last, he didn't have the first idea what to say to her.

Where did he begin?

"Er, I trust you slept well?"

Good Lord. Of all the places he might have started—apologies, and pleas for forgiveness—that was the best he could do? He'd hardly opened his mouth, and already he was making a mess of this.

"No. I slept very ill, indeed, but you didn't come all the

way here so early in the morning to ask me that, did you, Cass?"

Cass. Briefly, he closed his eyes. He didn't deserve her forgiveness, but as soon as she spoke his Christian name, he knew she'd already given it to him.

"No. I, ah..." He cast about for the right words to say, but in the end what emerged was a broken, "I'm so sorry, Hattie. Can you ever forgive me?"

She went still, the crunch of the graveled path under her feet going quiet.

"Forgive you? Cass, you *saved* me last night. There's no reason in the world for you to ask for my forgiveness. It's me who should be begging your pardon."

"No. I shouldn't have left you alone with Egerton. I know who and what he is. I should have been there, I should have—"

"I brushed off your warnings about him." Her fingers tightened on his arm. "You didn't do anything wrong, Cass."

He had. He'd done everything wrong, starting with ending their correspondence, and with it a friendship that meant more to him than anything else. He'd hurt them both.

"Your letters, Hattie. I know Egerton told you I showed them to him, but that's not—"

"Not true. Yes, I know. I never believed him for an instant. I know you would never show my letters to anyone, Cass."

Just like that, the weight that had been pressing down on him since last night fell away, and he could draw a deep, clean breath for the first time since last night.

Thank God, she hadn't listened to Egerton. Thank *God*.

"I would never do anything intentionally to hurt you, Hattie, but I was foolish enough to befriend Egerton, to trust him. I kept your letters in a locked drawer of my desk. But one night after an evening of debauchery he found the key and read some of them before I awoke and stopped him. I ended the friendship there and then, but the damage had already been done. After that, I realized how selfish I was. Your friendship with me was putting your reputation at risk—"

"Wait, Cass. That's why you stopped writing to me? Because Egerton found my letters?"

"Yes. If I hadn't been so thoughtless, he never would have known about them. I was afraid my friendship would end up hurting you."

"You never stopped caring for me, then. All this time I thought you found me dull, my life tedious, but those long months of silence were never about anything but your need to protect me."

He gave her a pleading look. "I never stopped caring about you, Hattie—"

"Hush." She pressed her fingers to his lips. "No more recriminations, Cass."

If she hadn't touched him it might have ended differently, but the moment she brushed her soft fingertips against his lips the dozen years they'd spent apart fell away as if they'd never been.

She'd been his first friend, the only one all those years ago who'd truly mattered to him. For those brief months in Kent, he'd had everything he ever wanted.

Nothing had changed since then. Now, twelve years later,

nothing mattered to him as much as she did. There was nothing in the world he wanted more than he wanted her.

When he looked at Hattie Parrish, he saw the future.

Everything else faded away in the face of that truth.

There was only one question left to ask, then.

What did Hattie see when she looked at him? Did she see her childhood friend, the boy she'd once crowned with daisy chains? Or did she see the man she'd grown to love?

It was as simple as that, in the end.

So, he took a deep breath, opened his mouth, and the words were already there, waiting for the chance to burst from his lips. "I'm in love with you, Hattie Parrish."

She went still. "Cass," she whispered, her blue eyes bright with tears.

"I've been in love with you for years." He took her hand and brought it to his lips. "There has never been anyone for me but you."

FOURTEEN

H er eyes were the deep blue of a thousand oceans at once, the morning sun behind her lighting up her fair hair like a golden halo, and it was everything Cass could do not to fall to his knees for her.

But Hattie was no angel, and neither was she the child from his memories. She was a living, breathing woman, one who needed to be kissed.

Often, and only by him.

But not yet, when everything remained unresolved between them still, and not here in the middle of Lady Fosberry's rose garden, not when her ladyship or Hattie's sisters might come searching for them at any moment.

He sucked a frantic breath into his lungs, his heart dancing wildly behind his ribs, and waited for her to decide his fate.

"I lied to you, Cass. I didn't come to London for the lecture or for Sir Joseph, or for the season." She took a step toward him and rested her hands on his chest, over his heart. "I came here for you."

He'd guessed it, but to hear the words from her lips was everything he'd ever needed. "Thank you, Hattie."

If she hadn't been so close, with the honeysuckle scent of her hair teasing his senses and the warm drift of her breath against his cheek, he might have been able to keep from touching her. But resistance was impossible in the face of such temptation, and logic and reason were no match for such overwhelming desire.

"I love you, Hattie." He brushed a golden tendril of her hair away from her cheek, his lips hovering over hers. "I'm yours, heart and soul. I've always been yours."

"Oh, Cass. I love you, too." She curled her fingers into his waistcoat, her blue eyes soft as she gazed up at him. "I thought...when you stopped writing to me, I thought you'd forgotten about me."

"No." He brushed his fingers over her lower lip, closing his eyes at the soft whimper that escaped her. "Never, Hattie."

"I..." She swallowed, her gaze dropping to his lips. "I missed you, Cass. When you left Kent, and every year afterwards, I missed you so much."

His hand drifted from the rosy silkiness of her lips to the white column of her neck and throat, his control slipping with every inch of her skin sliding under his fingertips. He wanted her, more than he ever thought he could want anyone, and for this one stolen moment, they were alone, and she was gazing up him at with sleepy blue eyes, as if she were waiting for him to kiss her...

One kiss. One kiss only, and then they'd go in search of Lady Fosberry.

Her lips parted, her kiss a gift for him alone. He took her mouth gently in a sweet, chaste kiss, but it wasn't enough. Nothing was ever enough with her.

"Hattie." He dropped an open-mouthed kiss behind her ear before trailing his lips lower, his tongue slipping out to taste the soft skin of her neck and teasing the fragrant hollow at the base of her throat.

"Oh, my. That's...it feels..." A soft, pleading sound left her throat as she twined her arms around the back of his neck, her fingers toying with his hair. "It makes me feel all shivery."

He chuckled, his lips brushing her earlobe. "Shivery is good, isn't it?"

"Yes, very good." She grasped his shoulders, her head falling back and hectic color blooming in her cheeks as he pressed another lingering kiss behind her ear.

"Look at me, Hattie." He caught her chin in a gentle grip and turned her face up to his, gazing down into blue eyes so wide and trusting he was overwhelmed with a tenderness that made his throat ache. "Let me see you."

She cast him a shy glance from under her lashes, her lower lip caught between her teeth, and God, he wanted to touch her everywhere, to stroke every inch of her soft skin until she was aching for him, writhing for him, her slender body taut in his arms. He wanted to pull every pin from her hair until those thick curls spilled into his hands like a golden waterfall.

He wanted to *see* her, to learn every alluring curve and

hollow of her, to lay her across the smooth silken sheets of his big bed, kiss her sweet pink nipples and taste the damp folds of skin between her legs until she was crying out for him, her hips undulating against his mouth as he brought her to climax.

He wanted to take her, here and now among the roses, their heady scent clouding his head and Hattie's cries echoing in his ears. She'd fall apart for him so sweetly, his name on her lips as she reached her peak with her hips moving in rhythm against his.

She was so soft, her mouth so soft and hot and open for him…

Just one more kiss. A final stolen kiss, then he'd take her back to the house.

He dropped damp kisses down the side of her neck until she was trembling for him, her eyelids heavy and her lips parted on a gasp, and it wasn't enough—no matter how much he had of her it would never be enough.

"We should return to the house, Hattie." Now, before he forgot he was meant to be a gentleman. "Lady Fosberry will be wondering where—"

She sank her fingers into his hair and gave a sharp little tug.

Cass groaned, his hips shooting forward at the delicious twinge of pain. Dear God, did she know what she was doing to him? She was driving him mad with her sweet, innocent caresses, the seductive press of her body against his.

"Hattie, we can't—"

"Shhh. We'll return to Lady Fosberry soon. Soon, Cass, but not yet."

He let out a defeated groan and nuzzled his face into the fragrant hollow of her shoulder, the faint hint of honeysuckle making him dizzy with desire. He would die if he didn't kiss her again.

Just one more kiss…

He caught her face in his hands, their breath mingling as he lowered his mouth to hers. The instant their lips touched the smoldering spark between them caught alight, and he tugged her closer, his arms closing around her waist.

It might have gone too far—it would certainly have gone too far if the crunch of carriage wheels coming up Lady Fosberry's drive hadn't penetrated his fogged brain.

Carriage wheels? Who would be visiting Lady Fosberry now? It was much too early in the day for callers, with the sun only having crested the horizon several hours earlier.

But there was indeed a carriage on the drive despite the early hour, a fine, navy blue one with gold fittings and shiny black wheels, and it was moving at such a brisk pace, the horse's hooves had kicked up a thick cloud of dust behind it.

"Oh, dear God." Hattie was watching the carriage's approach with wide eyes. "For pity's sake! Of all the hours in the day he might have arrived, why did it have to be right *now*?"

"Hattie?" Cass didn't recognize the carriage, but he'd caught a glimpse of a crest on the door. "Who is it?"

The carriage reached the top of the drive and came to a screeching halt in the circle at the bottom of the steps that led to the front door. One of the carriage doors flew open before the driver had a chance to descend from the box, and a tall gentleman in a handsome black greatcoat leaped out, a walking stick clutched rather threateningly in his gloved hand.

There was something familiar about him. Cass had seen this man before, but he couldn't quite place where he'd—

"Lord Windham!" The deep voice carried across the drive. "Be so good as to unhand my sister this instant, if you please! What do you mean, mauling her in the middle of Lady Fosberry's rose garden?"

His *sister*? "Er, Hattie, is that—"

"Yes, I'm afraid so." Hattie blanched as the man stalked across the drive toward the garden gate, every inch of him quivering with fury. "My brother Johnathan has arrived in London at last."

"Let me see if I have this straight." Johnathan paced to one end of the drawing room, paused, then marched back in the other direction, the heavy thud of his boots punctuating every word. "No sooner did—"

"Perhaps it would be best if you put your walking stick down, Lord Melrose," Lady Fosberry suggested calmly. "You wouldn't want to accidentally strike someone with it."

"Or not so accidentally," Sarah muttered under her breath, stealing a glance at Cass.

Johnathan ignored them and resumed his pacing. "No sooner did Emmeline and I leave for Oxfordshire than the three of you absconded to London without a word to anyone. Do I have that right?"

Hattie glanced at her sisters, but Margaret and Sarah

were both staring down at their hands as if they'd never seen anything as fascinating as their own fingers.

But it had been her idea to come to London, so perhaps it was only fair that she accept the brunt of Johnathan's wrath. "In a manner of speaking, yes, although I must say I think the word *abscond* puts it in a much uglier light than—"

"Imagine my shock when I ran into Lady Peregrine in Oxfordshire, and she told me what a delight it was to have met my charming sisters at Lady Featherington's garden party in London."

"Lady Farthingale's garden party," Sarah corrected. "Her name is Lady Farthingale."

"She may as well be Lady Rattletrap for all the difference it makes!" Johnathan threw his hands in the air. "I kept insisting to Lady Peregrine that she must be mistaken, that my sisters were in Kent until at last it dawned on me that perhaps you weren't in Kent, after all!"

"Oh, dear." Sarah wrinkled her nose. "How terribly embarrassing for you."

"Embarrassing?" Johnathan pinched the bridge of his nose between his fingers. "I didn't have the least idea my own sisters were in London!"

"Now, my lord," Lady Fosberry began in a soothing tone. "It's not as bad as you make it out to be."

"No? Forgive me, my lady, but I find it troubling indeed that my sisters left Melrose House without my permission! Without my knowledge, even! What in God's name were you thinking?"

"It's not as if we were here in London alone," Margaret

said. "Lady Fosberry has been taking very good care of us this entire—"

"That's another thing! You had no business involving Lady Fosberry in this wild scheme of yours!"

Lady Fosberry cleared her throat. "They did send me a letter asking for my assistance before they ever left Kent. It wasn't as if they ran off to London all willy-nilly—"

"Well, I'm pleased they informed someone of their plans, at least!" Johnathan paced to the window and back again before finally coming to a stop in front of the fireplace. "Do you have any idea what could have happened to you? Has it occurred to any of you all the things that might have gone wrong?"

"But nothing did go wrong, Johnathan," Lady Fosberry said in her most reasonable tone. "Your sisters are perfectly well, as you can see."

"I beg your pardon, but if nothing went wrong, then perhaps you'd care to explain why the first thing I saw when I came up the drive was Lord Windham kissing my sister in your rose garden!"

"Hattie!" Sarah's hand flew to her mouth, but there was no hiding the grin on her lips. "Kissing, in the garden! My goodness, how shocking of you! Wait until Alice Weatherby hears about—"

"Sarah, dear." Lady Fosberry shook her head. "Not now, if you please."

"I've heard some ugly rumors about you, Windham." Johnathan turned an icy glare on Cass. "I never credited any of them, because I remember you as a decent lad who was a good friend to my sisters, but now I wonder if the gossips weren't right about you all along, and you're every bit the scoundrel they—"

"Cass *isn't* a scoundrel!" Hattie leaped to her feet. "He's a good, decent gentleman."

"A good, decent gentleman doesn't take advantage of an innocent young lady by luring her into a deserted garden and—"

"Come now, Johnathan, that's not fair," Lady Fosberry began, only to be drowned out by Hattie. "For pity's sake, he never *lured* me any—"

"I'm in love with her, Melrose." Cass had remained respectfully silent throughout Johnathan's harangue, but now his quiet voice cut through the room, and every head turned towards him. "I've been in love with Hattie for years. I want to marry her."

Margaret let out a soft gasp before an abrupt silence fell.

But Hattie didn't notice it. She rose on shaking legs to face Cass, her heart melting at the tender expression in his dark eyes. "You...you want to marry me?"

"Of course I do, Hattie." Cass was at her side in an instant, reaching for her hands. "More than I've ever wanted anything."

"Why, how wonderful!" Sarah clapped her hands together with a squeal. "You're to become the Countess of Windham, Hattie!"

"I knew it all along." Lady Fosberry gave a satisfied nod. "Goodness knows it took you long enough to get on with it, Lord Windham. I was afraid Hattie would run off back to Kent before you could get to the point, but here we are."

"You must know, you must see how much I love you."

Cass brought her hands to his lips and kissed them, one after the other. "Will you have me, Hattie?"

A thousand words rushed to her lips at once, but in the end, to her everlasting shame she only got out a "Yes, please," before her eyes filled with tears.

"Then I have nothing more to wish for. You've made me the happiest of men, Hattie Parrish."

Cass pressed a chaste kiss to her cheek before turning and offering Johnathan a respectful bow. "I realize this is all a bit irregular, my lord, but I love your sister and would never do anything to hurt her. May I have your permission to have Hattie's hand in marriage, Lord Melrose?"

Johnathan looked from one smiling face to another and dropped onto a settee with a huff. "I suppose it's either a wedding or a duel, isn't it, Windham?"

They all held their breaths, waiting, until at last Johnathan let out a defeated sigh. "I'm not entirely sure about you, Windham, but you have my conditional blessing, pending a long betrothal in which you will endeavor to prove to me you're sensible of the treasure you've won. Do that, and I will be content."

"Oh, Hattie." Margaret rose to embrace her, tears in her eyes. "How happy I am for you! And Lord Windham." She turned to Cass, a tremulous smile on her lips. "I've always believed you and Hattie were destined for each other, ever since the first day you appeared in Kent."

"It does seem so, doesn't it?" Sarah jumped up and caught Hattie in a tight hug. "Fate is a strange creature, is she not? I only hope she's as kind to me and Margaret. Lady Blackhurst's rout is next week. Perhaps we should—"

"There will be no routs for any of you." Johnathan's lips were set in a stern line. "All three of you are returning to Kent with me as soon as the sun rises tomorrow morning. I suppose you're welcome as well, Windham," he added reluctantly.

Lady Fosberry exchanged a look with Margaret and Sarah. "Oh, no, I'm afraid that won't do, Lord Melrose."

"It won't do?" Johnathan looked from one to the other of them. "What do you mean, it won't *do*? Why the dev...that is, surely you don't expect me to return to Kent without my sisters? Emmeline is already beside herself with worry, and—"

"Hattie isn't the only one of your sisters with a suitor, Lord Melrose." Lady Fosberry gave him a bright smile. "Isn't it wonderful? Your sisters have taken the *ton* by storm this season."

"God help us all," Johnathan muttered.

"Lord Pembroke is courting Margaret, and he's ever so nice a gentleman, if a bit quiet, and Margaret quite likes him, don't you, Margaret?" Sarah turned to her elder sister with a mischievous grin. "Oh, look at that blush! She does like him!"

"Hush, Sarah, you naughty thing. Lord Pembroke is not courting Margaret. Not *yet*, in any case." Lady Fosberry turned to Johnathan. "But he's certainly taken with her, and I think he soon will be."

At this news, poor Johnathan looked even more befuddled than ever. "The three of you have only been in London for two weeks, and already there's one marriage proposal and an impending courtship?"

"A lady could do a great deal worse than Lord Pembroke."

Lady Fosberry observed. "He's an earl, and a respectable gentleman. His temperament suits Margaret's, as well. I know you don't wish to deprive your sister of a chance at happiness, my lord."

Johnathan rolled his eyes. "God forbid. If Margaret and Sarah wish to remain in London for the rest of the season, then I'm staying here, as well. I won't have all these scoundrels sniffing about my sisters like a pack of scandalous bees in search of honey. I'll send word to Emmeline as soon as—"

"I don't wish to remain in London, Johnathan," Sarah interrupted. "I'd much rather go to Staffordshire."

"Staffordshire!" Johnathan gaped at her. "But that's miles away! What in the world is there for you to do in Staffordshire?"

"Alice Weatherby's father, the Marquess of Aldridge has invited me to attend their house party as Alice's guest. They have one every year, and the invitations are highly coveted by the *ton*. All the most fashionable people attend. I may go, mayn't I, Johnathan?"

"A house party in Staffordshire with all the most fashionable members of the *ton*." Johnathan dragged his hand down his face. "What could possibly go wrong?"

"Lord and Lady Farthingale are going. They were kind enough to offer me a place in their carriage, and her ladyship promised to keep an eye on me. Please, may I go? Alice is my dearest friend, and it's been ages since I've seen her."

Johnathan glanced at Lady Fosberry, who gave him a quick nod, and with that, the battle was won. Johnathan doted on Sarah, just as they all did, and like the rest of them, he could refuse her nothing. "I suppose you may go."

"Oh, thank you!" Sarah rushed forward and pressed a kiss to Johnathan's cheek. "We couldn't ask for a better brother!"

"You're quite fortunate, indeed. Come, girls. We need to choose Margaret's gown for Lady Blackhurst's rout." Lady Fosberry beckoned to Sarah and Margaret, then raised an eyebrow at Johnathan. "Will you come, Lord Melrose?"

"To sort through Margaret's gowns?" Johnathan snorted. "No, indeed."

He strode over to the settee, but before he could sit down Lady Fosberry's gaze strayed to Hattie and Cass, and she gave Johnathan a little shake of her head.

"For God's sake." Johnathan let out a huff. "Very well. Five minutes, and Windham? I'll be right next door in the breakfast room. I can be back here in a matter of seconds. See that you don't give me any reason to return."

"Of course, my lord." Cass gave Johnathan a respectful bow, but a grin lingered at the corners of his lips, and his eyes were twinkling as they met hers.

Johnathan cast one final suspicious glance at them before disappearing through the door and leaving them alone at last.

"Have I told you, Lady Harriet, that you've made me the happiest of men?" Cass crossed the room and took her into his arms.

She gave him a teasing smile. "Not in the last half hour, no."

"Lady Harriet Parrish." He dropped a kiss onto the tip of her nose, his smile fading to something more tender as he drew back to look at her. "You've made me the happiest of men."

She rose to her tiptoes and pressed a soft kiss to his lips. "If we hurry back to Kent, do you suppose we'll arrive in time to see the last of the bluebells?"

"If not, we'll see them next year." He rested his forehead against hers. "We have all the time in the world to see the bluebells now."

EPILOGUE

CHATHAM, KENT, LATE JUNE 1819

"I don't recall this being quite so difficult last time." Cass fumbled with the crumpled stem in his fingers. "How are you managing it?"

"It's much easier for me." Hattie took his hand and pressed hers against it, palm to palm. "See? My hands are much smaller than yours."

"Hmm." He caught her wrist and tumbled her backwards onto the picnic blanket they'd spread out under the beech tree, sending the pile of daisies in her lap scattering. "Shall I take a closer look?" He brought her hand to his lips and pressed a kiss to the tip of each of her fingers.

"We'll never finish our daisy chains at this rate." But even as she scolded him, her hands stole around his neck, her fingers sinking into the thick mahogany locks of his hair. The severe *coup au vent* he'd been wearing when they'd first met in London had given way to a chaos of loose waves, and she could never resist running her fingers through them.

He turned onto his side to face her, his lips curving in the smile that made her heart leap like a wild thing in her chest. It was Cass's smile, the one she remembered from their first summer in Kent. The cold, aloof Earl of Windham's smile hardly ever appeared on his lips anymore.

He caught one of her curls between his fingers and lifted it to his lips. "May I steal a kiss, Lady Harriet?"

She pretended to consider it. "I don't know, my lord. Can you manage it without my brother seeing you? I could have sworn I saw him peering at us from his study window earlier."

Johnathan had come quite a long way in the month since Cass had come to stay with them in Kent. They'd even taken to sharing a glass of brandy in the evenings. Goodness only knew what they found to talk about behind the closed door of Johnathan's study. Masculine things, presumably, but she frequently heard laughter coming from within, so she was content.

"That, my dearest Lady Harriet," Cass said, cradling her cheek in his hand. "Is what the tree branches are for."

"Clever of you." She gazed up at him, her heart bursting with love in her chest as he lowered his mouth to hers, his tongue slipping out to tease her bottom lip.

She opened to him at once with a soft sigh, every inch of her skin leaping to attention under his wandering fingertips. He seemed to have been born with an innate understanding of her body, and with every week that passed it became more difficult to restrain themselves.

"Goodness," she murmured breathlessly when at last Cass raised his head. "Two weeks seems ages away, does it not?"

"It's an eternity." Cass pressed a final quick, hard kiss on her lips. "Thank God for this beech tree, or I don't know what we would have done."

Their wedding was two weeks from today, and it couldn't come quickly enough.

Margaret had returned to Kent from London only last week with a trunkful of Madame Céline's latest creations, a pronounced Town polish and elegance that had eluded her in Kent, and an offer of marriage from Lord Pembroke.

She'd accepted his suit and was to become Lady Pembroke a few short weeks after Hattie became Lady Windham. The tiny chapel on the Melrose House grounds would see two weddings this year.

So many changes, all at once! It hardly seemed possible she and Margaret would both be wed by the end of the summer. For Johnathan's sake it was rather a blessing that Sarah hadn't accepted any proposals. She never said so outright, but Hattie had a sneaking suspicion it wasn't due to a lack of offers.

Sarah had written faithfully from Alice's house party in Staffordshire, her every letter full of news and gossip. As it turned out, Lord Hayward had made certain the *ton* learned the truth about Egerton's brawl with Cass at Lady Dumfries's ball, and Egerton had been obliged to make a hasty retreat to his country estate to escape the whirlwind of gossip that followed.

Lady Laetitia hadn't fared much better. According to Sarah's last letter, the gossips had also found out about Lady Laetitia's part in the incident, and the rumors had been ugly enough that she'd ended her season without an offer, despite being this year's belle.

They'd hear it all firsthand, soon enough. Sarah would return to Kent next week, in plenty of time to see Hattie walk down the aisle.

"Do you suppose your brother will allow me to kiss you once we're married?" Cass grinned down at her. "Or should I expect him to toss me out a window when I attempt to follow you to our marital bedchamber?"

She twisted one of his curls around her finger. "Emmeline has promised me she won't allow it."

"That's reassuring." He flopped down beside her on his back, their hands clasped and his shoulder touching hers, and for some time they lay there quietly, watching the clouds skim across the patches of blue sky visible through the swaying branches above them.

Filtered sunlight spilled through the leaves, warming her face, and she closed her eyes, a contented sigh on her lips. How she'd miss Kent when they retired to Cass's estate in Oxfordshire!

But he'd promised her they would come to Melrose House whenever she wished it. She would miss her brother and Emmeline dreadfully, but they were often in Oxfordshire visiting her Aunt Juliet and her Aunt Helena, so she would see them often.

A shadow moved over her, and something brushed the end of her nose.

She opened her eyes to find Cass leaning over her, tickling her nose with a daisy dangling between his fingers. "Have I told you how lovely you look today, my lady?"

"You have, my lord." She tightened her fingers around his. "You tell me every day."

"As I should." His eyes darkened as he gazed down at her. "Because you're lovely every day. The loveliest lady in all of England."

The luckiest, as well. She was utterly smitten with her future husband, and why shouldn't she be? He was the dearest, loveliest and most handsome gentleman in the world.

She closed her eyes again, the shadows of the branches painting pictures behind her eyelids. How many hours had she spent under this very tree as a child?

It must be dozens. Hundreds, even.

This tree, the meadow with its rippling grass and the lazy pond was the place where she was happiest. It had always been so, but she'd never been happier than she was at this moment, lying under the beech tree with Cass, her fingers curled around his hand.

He was her past and her future, together.

How had she ever gotten so lucky?

"You're looking at me as if you want to kiss me, Lady Harriet."

"I always want to kiss you, Lord Windham." She reached up to brush her fingers across his lips. "Every moment of every hour, and every hour of every day."

He trailed his finger from the bridge of her nose to her lips, parting them with the gentle pressure of his thumb.

"Your every wish, Hattie..." He leaned closer, close enough his warm breath ruffled the loose tendrils of hair at her temples. "Is my command."

ALSO BY ANNA BRADLEY

Games Earls Play

Not Just Any Earl

Odd Earl Out

Fell in Love with an Earl

Earl Crazy

Here Comes My Earl

An Earl Like You

Christmas Novellas

Boughs of Folly

Then in a Twnkling

Tainted Angels

Standalone Titles

The Witching Hour

Other Series:

Besotted Scots

The Sutherlands

The Swooning Virgins Society

The Somerset Sisters

Sutherland Scandals

Drop Dead Dukes

ABOUT THE AUTHOR

Anna Bradley writes steamy, sexy Regency historical romance—think garters, fops and riding crops! Readers can get in touch with Anna via her webpage at http://www.annabradley.net. Anna lives with her husband and two children in Portland, OR, where people are delightfully weird and love to read.